CONCEALED
Passion

Lisa Horvath

iUniverse, Inc.
Bloomington

Concealed Passion

iUniverse books may be ordered through booksellers or by contacting:

iUniverse
1663 Liberty Drive
Bloomington, IN 47403
www.iuniverse.com
1-800-Authors (1-800-288-4677)

ISBN: 978-1-4620-3275-4 (sc)
ISBN: 978-1-4620-3274-7 (hc)
ISBN: 978-1-4620-3273-0 (e)

Library of Congress Control Number: 2011911151

Printed in the United States of America

iUniverse rev. date: 08/16/2011

To my husband,
for not only being the man I wake up with,
but the man I dream about.
To my son
who has taught me the true meaning of
love, passion, and joy.
To my family and dearest friends
for all their love and support,
and to Nana
for keeping my head on straight.
I love you all.

Torn between
The love of her husband,
Her beautiful child,
Her beautiful home,
She goes off to find herself.
Instead, she finds what she never
knew she lost,
Her sexuality.
No longer the feeling of a mom,
No longer the feeling of a wife,
But ultimately,
The feeling of a woman.

Rosalie Azzue

Prologue

The phone rang just after noon; I didn't have to look at the caller ID to know that it was my husband Matt. He always calls me at lunch.

"Hi," I answered.

"Hey, I just wanted to tell you I got next week off." Matt had requested the time but it wasn't approved until now.

"That's great! Anything else new or exciting?" I responded with happiness in my voice.

"No, I have a meeting through lunch so I have to go grab a quick bite. I'll talk to you later," he said abruptly.

"Okay, I love you."

"I love you too." He disconnected.

I hung up the phone and didn't know where to start. I sat on the couch just for a minute and took several deep breaths. Matt and I had been arguing over everything lately, and for the first time in our seven years of marriage, we went to see a counselor. Matt had returned to school six years ago and everything about us had changed. A kiss goodbye in the morning was all we had these last few years. He was married to his job and school. Being a stay at home mom was like having two full time jobs. That's what Dr. Phil says. Matt and I just weren't connecting anymore. I felt like sleep and fantasy football were more important to him on his free time, if he had free time. We were really struggling; we never talked about anything. It was easier to not say anything or just argue about it. The counseling was helping, but I was having a hard time believing any real changes would help. I didn't really know how I felt about him. I knew that I felt more alone now than ever in my life.

This weekend Matt and Hayden were going camping with the Cub Scouts. Hayden, my gorgeous four year old, had been looking forward to this time with his dad for so long. It hurt my heart that a man who slept here every night wasn't really home at all. His mind was either somewhere else or he was too tired to do anything. I felt bad most of all for Hayden. As he had gotten older, he waited for Matt to come home all day just to play something with him. We'd eat dinner and then Matt would fall asleep. What he didn't realize was the more he worked and had school, the more work I had. Only I didn't earn a paycheck.

I decided since they would be gone for the weekend, I'd take some time for myself. Our family owns a couple of condos on Panama City Beach. After our counseling session I realized that we could really use some time apart. I called my sister-in-law and asked if the condos were open. They were, and although I had the feeling she wanted to join me, I knew her life was too busy for her to get away. I really needed the time alone. Matt and I hoped that this time apart would help us appreciate each other more, and that we would miss each other enough to work through these times.

I had been on a self-help binge trying to lose a few pounds, working out more, and taking better care of myself. That was the trick, balance, which is really hard to do when you have to do everything yourself. This was the perfect reward! I was ready to have some time alone and just be myself. Not the maid, gardener or cook. Just me. It was Tuesday and they were leaving on Friday afternoon, which meant I had a lot to do.

1
Chapter

I had done my hair color, but went to a salon and had it trimmed, gave myself a manicure and pedicure, took a long bath last night and waxed everything. My skin felt smooth and silky. I packed everything I needed in one suitcase and everything I didn't in another. I guess that is a woman thing, we always pack things we might need. At two o'clock that afternoon I kissed Matt and Hayden goodbye and wished them a good time and off they went.

Hayden had been up every hour through the night asking if it was time to go. Just like Christmas Eve, my sister and I would knock on our parent's bedroom door every hour to see if it was time to open presents.

I walked back into the house and turned around to close and lock the door. I stood there for a moment and it was silent. A noise I hadn't heard in quite a while. I picked up all the Hot Wheel cars on the floor and cleaned up the kitchen. I pulled the Jeep out of the garage and put the top down. Matt had already put my suitcases in the Jeep earlier. I made sure I had my iPod and my sunglasses and closed the garage door.

It was a six hour drive north from where I lived in Pasco County to Panama City Beach, which meant I wouldn't get there until nine tonight. But I loved driving my Jeep, especially with the top down, feeling the wind and the freedom in the air. I put in my favorite blues album and sang every song, every word with a confidence that rarely showed itself. There was something about blues music that I had always related with, whether it was the music or the story of the song. After a few albums and my voice going hoarse from belting too loud, I turned off the stereo.

The weather in Florida is gorgeous this time of year. Even in October the temperature is in the high eighties. It was starting to cool off at night just enough to feel refreshing, still beautiful enough to enjoy the next week on the beach with a drink in my hand.

Maybe it was the quiet that surrounded me but I started to feel guilty, then I pushed the thought away. I'd miss my son so much, but I needed this. On top of having some marital difficulty, we also had a sink hole. The ground under our home was literally falling, taking our house with it. The damage was getting worse by the day. Lawyers, paperwork and the insurance company were all adding to my overall stress factor. I not only needed this time away, Matt still owed me from his bachelor party and a weekend in Vegas with the guys.

I'm not one to go out often, just the occasional scrapbooking night when all the ladies get together. Although we usually spent more time drinking wine than actually working on our scrapbooks, I really enjoyed time with the girls. Matt has been going out with the guys every Monday night for football since the season started, and I always stayed at home with Hayden.

I needed this vacation and wasn't going to try and justify it to myself anymore.

I was thinking too much so I turned the radio back on and scanned through central Florida radio stations. The song that was playing was "Brown Eyed Girl," and it reminded me of my dad. Two weeks ago his band had played in a "battle of the bands" at the bayou in Tarpon Springs and they won second place. Whenever I think of him I smile. I sang along and thought of how great my dad's band sounded. He looked so good up there and I was so proud of him. Through everything we had been through as a family, he was and still is always there for me. I wondered if I told him enough how much I loved him. He is retired now and is home all day. I love that I can just pick up the phone and know that he's always there, even if we just talk about the laundry. I always enjoy our conversations. Sometimes it seems like he's more my best friend than my dad but I wouldn't have it any other way.

It was just over the half-way point when I stopped to get some coffee and use the restroom. When we had gone to Panama City Beach before, we always stopped in this one town that has this great sandwich shop. It felt weird going somewhere by myself. I had never been away from Hayden for more than a couple of hours and was already missing him at my shirt tails.

I went to use the bathroom, and when I looked at myself in the mirror as I washed my hands, I started to cry. It was something I did a lot in the last few months. I fixed my wind-blown hair and wiped the tears from my eyes. I stood back and looked again in the mirror. My hair was brown, almost bronze with highlights from the sun. My eyes were brown and usually blood shot from crying. I was only five foot four, but muscular from all my years in sports and working out. I loved my skin, dark with the Indian red hue. When I smiled it showed off my perfect white teeth and the five dimples on my cheeks. I had always thought I looked good, even now, going on forty. I just couldn't understand why my husband wasn't attracted to me anymore, or why I felt so low on his list of priorities.

I wiped my eyes again and walked out of the restroom. I grabbed my coffee and headed back out to my Jeep. The rest of the drive went quickly as I sang and let my thoughts go free.

I pulled up to the front of the tall building and took another deep breath. We had been here several times before, a couple of summer vacations and a holiday here and there. Some of the visits were wonderful and some not so much. The valet came around and opened my door, as I slowly got out and stretched my legs. He had already gotten my suitcases out. I handed him my keys and insisted I could manage by myself. If I was anything, I was stubborn.

The condos here were million dollar investments, mostly rented out for a pretty penny. The location was prime, smack dab on the emerald coast beach. It seemed more like an exclusive resort than a building of condos. The customer service was absolutely pampering. They were just a phone call away from anything you needed or wanted. As I walked through the lobby at least four people asked if they could help me. I took the elevator to the fifth floor and with my key card in hand stood at the door. I punched in the code on the door to make sure it was the same, in case I forgot the key card if I went out.

I opened the door and as I walked inside I was immediately drawn to the view directly across the open living room to the balcony. I dropped my suitcases and walked to the railing outside. With my eyes shut, I inhaled a deep breath of the salty breeze. Something about the sun and sea made the goddess come out in me.

I remember growing up at the beach with my family. We would spend all day there during the summers. The beach was like a sensual spa to me sharing the sounds, the smells, and feelings that made me feel sexy and alive. Like a good lover, taking pleasure in giving pleasure. I've clearly been reading too many romance novels.

My excitement obviously made its way to my right foot and I arrived earlier than expected. It was only eight thirty p.m. and I didn't want to just go to bed. Not this week. I called Matt to let him know I had gotten to the condo safely. Usually my phone doesn't get a signal here, but I got through.

I unpacked all my essentials from my suitcases and slipped into a hot bath. RELAX! I really wanted a glass of wine but didn't feel like going to the store for groceries tonight. I dressed in a casual sundress, touched up my make-up and fluffed my hair. Having a Jeep requires having a hairstyle that looks good all messed up. Tiki bar here I come. I threw on a silk wrap I had brought in case it was cool outside, and I headed downstairs.

The bar was outside; they had a band playing tropical music with those steel drums. I loved that. Not many people were here for a Saturday night, but this was not the season for vacationers. Only six tables were taken and a few people were standing at the bar. I walked to the table in the corner and sat with my back toward the building so that I could enjoy the moon and its reflection on the ocean.

The waiter walked over with a glass of water and asked me what he could get for me. I was asking him questions about the specials when I noticed a stain on his tie. His name tag said "Tony." As he was telling me the drink specials, I automatically grabbed the napkin on the table, dipped it in my glass of water, and started rubbing his tie. He stopped talking and looked down at me like I was insane. I realized what I was doing and laughed at myself.

"I'm sorry. I am such a mom. At least I didn't lick my finger and wipe your face." We both laughed and I felt extremely embarrassed. I ordered a glass of Pinot Grigio. The waiter walked away and I leaned my head back on the chair and closed my eyes. I felt aroused, alive. I sat taking in the music and the soft breeze on my face.

I started thinking about Matt and the problems we'd been having. At our last counseling session, I wasn't even sure we had enough to hang on to. I thought our foundation was stronger. All I wanted was him to be home more, to want to be home. I was willing to give up my Jeep, move to a smaller house, anything so that he didn't have to work as hard and could be home with us. The material things had never mattered to me. I just wanted him to want me the same way.

I was starting to wonder where they had to go to get the wine. It seemed like forever. When I opened my eyes the waiter was coming to my table. He put a bottle and two beautiful goblets on the table.

"Compliments of this gentleman." He motioned his hand in the direction of the bar. There was one man by himself sitting at the end of the bar. I nodded in thanks and the waiter poured my glass.

I turned my attention back to my table, thinking to myself about how uncomfortable that was. Maybe that's what they do these days. It's been a long time since I've dated. Before I met Matt, it was one blind date after another. I never really picked someone myself. Even Matt was a blind date, but he stole my heart instantly.

I started looking around the outside bar. Several couples sat close together at their table. I smiled if they caught me looking. There was a large table with six men dressed in polo shirts and shorts, eating and chatting. I wondered if they had a business meeting or convention. Three people were standing at the bar together talking, laughing and flirting. Then, there was one man, sitting by himself, at the other end of the bar. I wondered how he could sit with his back to this magnificent view behind him. He was looking at the doors to the building. His hair was medium brown, slightly wavy, and hung just above his shoulders. His skin was russet and beautiful next to the light colored clothing he had on. His eyes looked brown from where I was sitting. He had on a cream colored linen shirt unbuttoned just enough to see his chest. Hmm, no hair. His pants were the same color linen and pressed. Hard to keep that way, when it comes to linen. Maybe he just got here. I looked at his shoes, nice, and then I raised my gaze back to his face. He was looking at me. How embarrassing. I wondered how long he had watched me looking at him. I bent my head down and closed my eyes. A giddy kind of feeling made me smile. I opened my eyes, reached for my glass and took a sip. Knowing forty was only a few months away, this was making me feel young and sexy. Anything that boosted my ego at this point was welcome. Taking another sip of wine, not paying attention to anything, just my thoughts, I hadn't noticed that he had gotten up and was walking to my table until I saw him out of the corner of my eye. I felt crippled. I wanted to get up and walk away, but my body wasn't moving. Now it was too late.

"May I join you?"

"Of course, please, and thank you for the wine. It's wonderful."

"My name is Rafael." He extended his hand.

"Maya." I gave him my hand; he kissed it and let it go. Oh my God! What was he doing? I'm sure from where he was sitting at the bar that he could see my wedding ring. As he sat down, I looked down at my wedding ring. It was three generations. The diamonds in my wedding band were from my mother's wedding ring, and the diamonds in the engagement ring were from my grandmother's wedding band. Matt and I only picked the center stone and had it made. When Hayden was ready, it would be his to remake and add to. It was too beautiful not to pass on and share what it meant to those who wore it.

I looked up and he was staring into my eyes. If my skin wasn't so tan, he would see me blushing.

"What brings you to this glorious place tonight?" He looked at the empty glass beside the bottle and asked, "Do you mind?"

"I'm on vacation." I picked up the bottle of wine and poured it in the second glass. He had a very sexy accent and it was clearly from a Spanish speaking country.

"Thank you." He held his glass up to make a toast and said, "To vacations!"

I touched my glass to his and when I caught his eyes, there was the same look of torment and sadness I saw in my own eyes when I looked in the mirror. We sat for a while not saying anything at all which was good because I didn't really know what to say. I finished my glass of wine and would have looked at my watch if I wore one.

"Would you like to dance?"

"I'm married."

"It's just a dance, and you're on vacation, right?"

He reached out his hand and I stood up, ignored his hand and walked passed him toward the little area open for people to dance. Only one other couple was dancing, and luckily there weren't many people still here. What am I doing? I have had to remind myself ten times in the last hour why I am here, and just try to relax and enjoy. I wanted to do things that I don't get to do at home. I wanted to dance, I wanted to get a henna tattoo, go shopping, drink too much and just enjoy freedom.

We stood in front of each other, and I took his left hand with my right hand then put my arm on his shoulder. He reached around my waist and pulled me closer. Too close. The heat from his body gave me the goose bumps and sent a shiver down my spine. His breath on my neck was hot. With every breath he took against my skin, I felt my body relax, like singing a lullaby to a child. He spun me around and back into his arms, closer to his body than before. I felt his erection against my hip.

"I'm sorry. I think it's time to say good night. Thank you for the dance and the wine."

I walked away from him and went back to the table to get my purse and headed for the doors. The elevators were right inside and I pushed the button to go up. As I stepped in the elevator, he stepped in behind me and I pushed the button for my floor.

"Are you following me?" I asked him brusquely.

"Actually no, I am staying on the fifth floor also. Besides I only stayed outside because of you. Now that you are leaving, I might as well get some work done."

The elevator opened and we both got out.

"Good night then," I said quietly as I walked to the condo door, and when I reached for the key, I noticed he was staying in the condo next to me. Great. Now what?

2
Chapter

I went inside the condo and locked the door. What are the odds of him staying right next to me? I shook my head and walked toward the master bedroom. I had never stayed in this room. When we'd come before, Matt, Hayden, and I all slept in the second bedroom while my brother and sister-in-law stayed in the master bedroom. My nephews slept in the bunk beds in the entry hall or the pull out sofa. The master was gorgeous. It was at the back of the condo overlooking the beach and ocean. It had a large Jacuzzi tub with separate shower and more counter space than I had at home.

There was a knock at the door. I walked to the door with anxiety spilling from my pores, and stupidly opened the door thinking that it was the man next door. It wasn't. Before I could say anything, these two huge Latin-looking goons pushed me inside and I fell on my butt. They invited themselves in and locked the door behind them. I've never been in a situation that required screaming before and wasn't sure I could now.

"Who the hell do you think you are?" I said with attitude, but I thought they deserved it.

"Sit the hell down and we'll explain everything."

"Maybe you haven't noticed but I am sitting down, thank you very much. Now please tell me what is going on." These guys were so big, they looked like WWF wrestlers. They were huge looking down at me still sitting on the floor. I stood up, walked to the couch and sat down.

"Where is your purse?"

"Why?"

"Just go get it and bring it to me."

I went to the bedroom, grabbed my purse and threw it at him. I wondered what he wanted with it. He opened it and went through everything, which wasn't much because I only carried my wallet, lipstick and keys in it.

"If that shade of lipstick doesn't work for you, I brought a few others." Again attitude, something my husband thinks I need to work on. I'm starting to see that.

"What do you know about the man you danced with downstairs?"

"His name is Rafael." I started to think about his name. Of course it was Rafael, looking the way he looked. Body hard and muscular, dark skin, brown hair that hung just above his shoulders, beautiful features and an accent that would make women weak in the knees, hot.

"What else?"

"That's all, is there something I should know about him?"

"I can tell you are not going to make this very easy," the arrogant one announced.

The other one never said a word. Did I mention they were huge? Like six foot five huge, and it was obvious lifting weights was a job requirement.

"We were hoping you would be a little more cooperative."

"What is this all about?" They clearly had the wrong person here; I was sure they would figure it out and just leave.

"The man downstairs has something we want and you're going to get it for us."

"What would that be?"

"A flash drive. He has it on him or in his room and you are going to get it for us."

So that's what he wanted my purse for, to see if Rafael had put this flash drive in my purse.

"And how am I supposed to get it?"

He held out his phone to me, and I took it and looked at him. I said "Hello." It was my sister crying. She said, "Just do what you have to do so we can go home."

The call disconnected. I handed back the phone, and the talkative goon gave me some ugly face as if to say 'so there'. I rolled my eyes. I made a quick decision and thought the best course of action was to remain calm and nonchalant.

"You two aren't the smartest men I've met. If you are trying to use my sister as leverage to get what you want, I'll have to think about it." Idiots should have known that my sister and I were never that close. We fought all the time, always had. They should have picked a better hostage if they really wanted leverage. I wondered how the hell they had gotten my sister so quickly, but I stayed silent. Then I realized that I was automatically protecting the man that was in the condo next to me. The man I danced with tonight. The man that made me feel alive inside again. I could have told them where he was, but I didn't.

"If you don't get the flash drive before he hands it over to his contact, I'll kill your sister first and you can watch. Do you understand?"

"Yes." She was my sister. I started to wonder if she was mixed up in this somehow. She always had a way of finding trouble if it didn't find her first.

"Great, I'm glad we understand each other. We will be watching you, so behave yourself."

They walked out the door the same as they walked in, loud and rude. I sat there wondering what I was supposed to do next and where my sister was. Well, this was really putting a damper on my plans for the next week, and who knew how much time I had to find this flash drive. I didn't even know when these two hired men would show up again.

I remembered something I had packed in one of my suitcases and went to find it. I found out that this little gas station I stopped at earlier this week sold the synthetic marijuana that had been all over the news and bought two packets and a pack of rolling papers. I stuck them in a Ziploc bag and tucked it in one of my folded shirts. I got out the bag. Went out to the kitchen, picked up the phone, and ordered a bottle of wine from the bar downstairs and told them to add it to Rafael's bill. It wasn't that I didn't have the money, it was just the principle. I was pissed. I just wasn't sure who I was so mad at.

I waited for the wine then went out to the balcony to enjoy my wine and rolled some of the leaves from the packet into a cigarette. I thought it would be fun to try it knowing that this week was about me and not having any responsibilities. I had smoked pot years ago at a party here and there and wanted to see what it was like. I sat silently, but my mind was going in a million directions. What was I supposed to do? An hour went by and my thoughts were overwhelming me. I couldn't stop thinking about my sister, Shelby, and what she must be going through. I needed to take a walk. Barefoot, I stepped out of the condo and the door locked automatically as it closed.

The view from the front was of the street with all the lights from surrounding businesses, but there was no traffic or people walking. In season the streets would be full of cars, rental scooters, and people everywhere.

I'm sure it was the wine in me that made me stop at the door next to mine and I knocked. He opened the door, no shirt on, just the linen pants, no shoes. I was blushing again or maybe just distraught. It didn't matter.

"Hi, again, I was just a little restless and was going to go for a walk on the beach. Would you like to come with me?"

He looked down and saw I didn't have shoes on either, then looked up and smiled.

"I could use a break."

Okay, I had just asked this man out. I really had no idea what I was doing.

We walked along the shore of the beach and after what seemed like ten minutes, I stopped and sat down on one of the cabana chairs that are rented out during the day. I needed some answers and I didn't know who to talk to or who I could trust.

"Who are you?" I knew his name but nothing else.

"I told you my name is Rafael."

"Who are you really? When I got back to my condo, two men came in and apparently you have something they want, and I'm supposed to get it or they are going to kill my sister."

Chapter 3

"I know who they are. They've been here doing surveillance on me for two days. My team and I work for a government agency, special operations. His expression was sad as I looked at him. "I'm so sorry," he said.

"Sorry?"

"I saw you come outside earlier and I should have just left you alone, but I was so drawn to you. This is my fault."

"Tell me what to do," I said almost begging.

"Well as you know they don't have a brain between them. They are looking for a flash drive that has already been handed over to my superior. We have been tracking them and all of their communications. We'll find your sister. In the meantime, I'm afraid we're both just going to have to play along. I promise you this will all work out."

For some reason I believed him. Then I wondered about the sadness I saw in his eyes the first time I saw him sitting at the bar. He was facing me, sitting on another chair. He raised his hand up and brushed my face with his fingers. I wasn't blushing anymore. If there were a chance that I was going to be killed by him or the other goons, having a romantic, exciting fantasy come true with a chance of some adventure would be on my "bucket list", and I could definitely cross that off. It is what it is, that's what my husband always says. Then I looked away as a flood of family images came to mind, then I looked back into his eyes.

"What about my husband and my son?"

"We will have people watching them every second. They will be safe, and they probably don't know anything is going on."

"But they aren't at home; they went camping and won't be home until Sunday afternoon."

"You have to trust me."

"Are you kidding me? Thugs are holding my sister hostage, my family could be in danger, I don't even know if I'll live through this, and I'm supposed to trust you. I don't even know you."

He took my hand and we walked along the shore. It seemed like forever, but when I turned around I could still see the building where I was staying. He stopped and turned with me to see what I was looking at, and when our eyes met again, he pulled me close to him and with the softest lips I had ever felt, he kissed me. He gently touched his lips to mine, and then harder. I put my hand to his bare chest breaking the connection and for the first time since leaving his condo door, I allowed myself to look at his chest, his muscles, and his smooth skin. I noticed my touch made his nipples hard. He had his hand on my lower back and pulled me in for another kiss. I felt his breath, I felt his lips, and between the sensation of heat and the wine, I knew I was in trouble. With one arm around my waist and his other hand on the side of my head, I parted my lips and kissed him in return. When that sweet kiss ended, I put my head on his chest. Silence again, not just from my own thoughts or worries, but a silence that required nothing.

I thought about nothing at first, then I went numb. I hadn't felt wanted in so long, the sheer attraction was pulling me in.

We walked back in the direction of our building and reached the bar outside. I sat on a stool and he sat next to me. I ordered a shot of whiskey and a glass of red wine. He ordered the same. We tapped our glasses together, downed the shots and put the empty glasses on the bar.

Rafael took the phone from his pocket and pushed one button. He looked at me and excused himself while he stood up from the stool and walked a few feet away. I watched him pace back and forth while he talked on the phone. My husband did the same thing. After a few minutes, he walked back over to the stool and sat down.

"We are putting cameras and microphones in your condo. We'll be able to monitor you at all times. My team swept for bugs and it came up clean. I know they will be watching us. As soon as we can get a location on your sister, this will all be over. It looks like they used your phone to find her."

"How?"

"The last number dialed on your phone was to a disposable phone. The call before that was to your sister."

"Okay, how did they get to her?" I was confused.

"I don't know yet, but we are going to do everything we can to get her back safely."

I really didn't know what I was supposed to say. I didn't really have many options at this point. I wondered what my sister's husband was thinking right now. Their son always spent the weekends at his grandmother's house, so at least they didn't have to worry about him right now. So many thoughts started popping into my head, crowding it with fear and anxiety until Rafael broke the silence.

"Do you want me to stay with you tonight?"

"No, I'll be fine. Where are the cameras in my condo?"

"In every room except the master bedroom and bathroom. There are also microphones in the basket of shells on the coffee table and one at the entry. If you need anything, just ask. "

So the only privacy I had was in the master suite. At least he left me that. Remind me not to talk to myself. I looked down at the bar and stared at my glass of wine. We sat quietly for a few minutes and then Rafael asked,

"Why are you here alone on vacation, if you don't mind my asking?"

I turned my head to look at him.

"My husband and I are having some problems and I wanted to have some time to decide what I wanted to do. We've been seeing a counselor, and I'm just not sure that we can work things out. I don't want to stay together if we aren't happy together. I'm worried about our son. I can't believe I'm telling you all of this." I looked back to my wine and took a sip.

"I'm sorry you are unhappy. I have no right to ask, but how could any man not be happy with you?" He looked with an inquisitive face.

I shook my head.

"You don't even know me." I was still looking at my wine glass and didn't want to look at Rafael. I felt his hand touch mine and he held it in his. I felt the tears well up in my eyes and I needed to stop them from falling. I needed to think about something else before I just fell apart. This was just the last thing that I needed to deal with right now.

We finished our wine and returned to our own condos. Nothing else was said. I closed the door and locked it. I went to the large flat screen TV and turned it on, went in the bedroom, closed the door, and sat on the edge of the bed. I didn't cry. I just sat there looking at the floor. I had wondered for the last few years how anything could be more important to Matt than his family. I felt so sad and more alone than ever. I loved him dearly and couldn't understand how we got so far off track. I thought like every other woman that love and marriage would withstand anything. I've never thought of myself as naïve, but I was questioning if love was enough. After about thirty minutes of thinking about Matt and the situation with my sister, I curled up on the pillow and fell asleep.

Chapter 4

I woke up facing the window and saw the light from the early sun reflecting off the water. I felt warm and comfortable. I sat up in bed and hoped I had just had a really crazy dream. I took my clothes off to get in the shower, but I needed coffee first. I headed to the kitchen and started the pot brewing, then walked back to the shower. My things were already in their places like I lived here.

"Oh my……" I froze where I stood in the bathroom and remembered that Rafael had cameras in every room. I just walked through the whole place naked. I looked up to the ceiling and then beyond, begging for a sign, or forgiveness. I wasn't sure.

I put a robe on when I got out of the shower and went for the coffee. I took it out to the balcony and held the cup between both hands. It was a little cool outside and the hot coffee made me feel warm all over. There were French doors that opened from the bedroom to the balcony. I went to my suitcase and pulled out a pack of cigarettes. I quit smoking a few months ago, but this was a vacation, right? Not only that but my nerves were shot as I thought of all the things that happened last night. I smoked a cigarette with my coffee and enjoyed the beautiful sky. I didn't even bother wondering about the time. I had a week, a week that would be nothing like I could ever imagine. A sudden "knock knock" at the door startled me, and I almost dropped my coffee. I sat it down on the table and warily went to the door.

"Who is it?" I'd learned my lesson last night not to open the door without knowing who was on the other side. My butt still aches from that.

"Breakfast, Senora."

"I didn't order any breakfast." I knew it was him by his voice.

"Breakfast with Rafael, Senora."

I opened the door and he wore a huge smile. I was sure it was the clear naked view I gave him earlier, but I didn't mention it. He didn't either. He was carrying a tray and pulled the top off to reveal an assortment of fruit, cheeses and pastries. I shook my head in disbelief and opened the door for him to come in. He went into the kitchen, poured himself a cup of coffee, and headed out to the balcony. I followed him. We both sat at the table and starting picking from the tray.

"If they don't have surveillance in here, why are you doing this?"

"Because they are watching, and because I can protect you better if I'm with you."

"That's not what I was talking about." I wanted to know if this was part of his job, the show we were supposed to be putting on, or if there was more to it.

"Why me?"

"My team and I were supposed to leave yesterday, but we really liked it here. We had been on this assignment for weeks and needed a break, so we decided to stay a few more days. It's my fault you're in this mess. If we would have left"…he paused "the two hired guns would know that the exchange of the flash drive had already taken place and would have seen us leave. When you walked out to the bar last night, I thought I'd never seen such beauty and sexuality. You looked so strong and confident. You took my breath away. Everything about you excites me. Your hair, your eyes, your body and the way you move. Your skin is like gold and bronze, soft and warm, like if you could touch the sunset right before it vanished. When I saw you talking to the waiter and then wiped his tie, you made me smile. When you laughed, it made me laugh. No one has ever made me feel that way."

I saw the look in his eyes again with the hint of sadness and torment. I wondered why my husband didn't feel the same way about me like this mysterious man I just met. I needed to feel wanted. I wanted to feel needed. Rafael was definitely making me feel both. A complete stranger was making me feel attractive.

I was really glad I took the time to pamper myself before I got here. I wouldn't feel this sexy right now if my toes looked the way they did last week.

"I was heading down to the beach. I suppose you'll be joining me, if it's safer, I mean."

"Only if you want me too." He looked at me like he was hoping I wanted him to.

I nodded coyly, barely moving my head.

"I'll get ready and meet you downstairs."

He got up and walked out without saying anything more. I guessed the less I knew the better. At this point, quiet was good.

I finished messing up my hair with the blow dryer and put on a new tankini I bought for the trip with a matching sarong with vivid blues and browns and gold swirls throughout the material. I put some gloss on my lips and packed my bag of beach goodies.

When I arrived downstairs I didn't see him, so I walked to a spot close to the water. I laid my blanket down, unfolded my little chair and sat my bag down. I turned around and stood looking at the ocean, the breeze blowing gently, I leaned my head back and closed my eyes. I felt him getting close to me. I could smell him. I felt his hands on my shoulders and him touching my skin, his hands moving slowly down my arms until he reached my hands. He grabbed my waist and slowly turned me around to face him. I thought I was going to faint. I haven't been touched in that way in years. I almost wanted to cry. He lifted my chin and asked,

"Would you like something to drink?"

"I'd love something cold and alcoholic." I'm sure by now he knew that I charged that bottle of wine last night to his bill.

"I'll be right back."

I sat in my chair and pulled out a book I'd been reading, as if my mind could focus on words right now. I'd pretend for show at least so it wasn't completely obvious that I was shaking. He returned with two beers and sported a pair of cargo shorts, showing me everything that wasn't covered. Thankful I had sunglasses on I looked him over again as he walked toward me. It was dark last night when I saw him without his shirt on. Now in the bright sun it was easier to see the beauty in his body. His shoulders wide and strong, every muscle defined, and his incredible legs. He sat down on the blanket I had lain down on the sand and handed me a bottle of beer with a lime sticking out of it. It reminded me of my brother-in-law; he always drank this brand of beer with a lime.

"Thank you." I squeezed the lime, shoved the rest into the bottle and took a sip.

"My pleasure."

"So since you work for some government agency, I'm sure you have a thick file on me. What do you know?"

"I know that you charged a bottle of wine to my account last night. I know that you don't have any tan lines, and I know you are a stay at home mom and adore your family."

We both smiled at each other. But I'm sure it was for different reasons.

My cell phone rang. Incredible! I have never gotten service here before, not even one bar, and now it works. That's great. I noticed the phone number was blocked on the display and answered it. It was the talkative goon. All he said was, "You are running out of time." Then he hung up. I threw the phone on the blanket next to my bag.

"Who was it, Maya?" Rafael asked with a concerned face.

"The rude man from last night. He said I was running out of time and then hung up."

"Come lie next to me. I'm sure they are here watching."

I did what he said. This was a little out of my league. If you needed a button sewn on or some flowers pruned, I was your woman. Then, very softly, he whispered to me,

"Roll on top of me, grab my phone from my waist and put it in my hand."

I had no other choice but to trust him, so I did exactly that. I didn't want to ask too many questions. I didn't want to know what this was all about. I just wanted my sister back unharmed and my family safe. He was laying on his back with his arms above his head. I grabbed his phone and swung my right leg over his body at the same time. I felt the bulge in his pants between my legs. I reached above his head to hand him the phone and my face was an inch away from his. He quickly rolled over so that he was on top of me with our hands still connected over my head. He kissed my neck, slowly and so passionately. I was at his mercy. He whispered in my ear that he was going to sync the information on my phone to his. I didn't even know you could do that. He moved his kisses to my mouth, and I knew he felt my heart beating fast and hard. He rolled off to his side, facing me, with one hand holding his head up and the other grabbing for his beer. He smiled that smile, a sneaky smile.

"I think we could use a couple more beers," he said as if he were talking to me.

I started to get up, and he grabbed my hand and pulled me back down.

"One of my team will be here in a minute; she'll bring the beers and take my phone. Maybe we can get something from the phone call."

A minute later, a woman dressed in a waitress uniform strode over with our drinks.

"They can hear you?" I knew from the movies and books that I had read that there were many little earpieces and microphones that secret agents use to communicate.

"Yes."

I turned to lay on my stomach and faced his direction. I just stared into his eyes, which in the sun didn't look brown at all. Only the outside rim was brown with green, hazel and gold nestled together. They were beautiful. I wondered why they looked so troubled, but then I didn't know anything about him.

Chapter 5

I must have dozed off looking at him, because when I opened my eyes, there was a straw hat over my face, blocking the sun. He was still laying there looking at me. I sat up wondering how long I was asleep. I never knew what time it was at home during the day. I wasn't going to start worrying about the time now.

"Did your team get anything from the phone call?"

"They have a range of the location where they have your sister. It tells us he didn't call from here, but that doesn't mean others aren't watching. My team is narrowing down the location, then they'll begin the surveillance."

Those sad eyes again.

"Why do you look so sad?"

"I'm really sorry that I got you involved in this mess. It's my fault. I feel terrible, but the time I have spent with you has made me want more out of my life than this job. You make me want to be a better person and have a family. I read some things in your file and they made me want to have someone like you in my life."

"So you've never thought of having a normal life?"

"Not until now."

"Did your team hear all of that?"

"Yes."

"Wow! Are your devices waterproof?"

"No."

"Then I suggest that you take them off and come in the water with me. I'm hot from laying out here, my beer is warm and I think it's time to cool off and get wet." Not like I wasn't hot and wet already.

I walked toward my favorite part of the beach where the water comes up to the sand and washes away again. The tide was low and for some reason made me think of my marriage and how the tides are like passion. Coming in high at times and then going out so far, putting distance between the shore and the sea. I was definitely feeling the distance and low tide in my marriage.

As I entered the water I felt so sexy and beautiful from the things that Rafael said and did. I wasn't sure what was going to come next.

I started to wonder how Matt and Hayden were doing. Camping wasn't Matt's favorite activity. There were not cabins with beds and full kitchens in the Cub Scouts. I was sure that Matt was feeling way out of his league out in the woods. I was in Girl Scouts for years and camping was always my favorite part. I should have gone with all the boys to show them how it was done!

I turned around and saw Rafael getting up from the blanket. I wondered what he was doing. I walked out far; it was shallow for a good fifty feet and then started to get deeper. I stopped about waist deep and bent my knees to get water to my shoulders. The water was cool and wonderfully refreshing. I didn't see Rafael. Then I felt something touch my leg. I jumped and he came up from under the water with a sneaky smile on his face.

"What took you so long?"

"I figured you might be hungry, so I ordered a platter of fresh fruits and some champagne."

"Aren't you thoughtful?" I looked around and there was only one other couple on the long stretch of private beach, and they weren't paying attention to anyone but each other.

I'd never seen this place so quiet.

Rafael reached for my arms and put them around his neck. He wrapped his arms around my waist and pulled me so close to him. I stared at him, afraid, anxious, and definitely aroused. He pressed his lips to my shoulder and moved toward my neck, then to my ears. He held his face so close to mine I could feel his breath, taste the beer. The buds on the tip of my tongue were tingling. I felt one of his hands move to the front of my waist and down to the front of my bathing suit. He slid the material to the side and brushed his finger along the center of me and moved it up and down so slowly. I moaned from my stomach to my throat. Purely electric, I felt like I could light up New York City for a week. His lips touched mine and he played with them, licking them and sucking them. His tongue found mine and they danced together, tasted each other, and each fought for the other. His kisses turned more passionate, and I was feeling every part of my body growing tense. His finger slid inside me, and I instantly felt my climax coming quickly. I broke my lips away from his and leaned my head back in absolute astonishment. I rode on the edge as long as I could and finally released my every inhibition, sounds I have never uttered coming out of my mouth. He was kissing my neck and brushing his lips against my skin as he felt every muscle tighten and then slowly relax. It took several minutes to regain focus. I turned my head down to see his eyes, and he pulled me against him. I felt his erection and was surprised when he starting rubbing himself against me. We kissed so deeply and I was climaxing again from the friction of his body against mine. I felt exhausted, like I had just run on the treadmill for an hour. I collapsed in his arms and rested my head on his chest. I heard his heart beating as fast as mine. We didn't talk at all. We just stayed in the water in each other's arms. I couldn't move. I didn't want to move. Finally, he asked me,

"Are you hungry?"

"Yes." Now I was the one with few words.

We walked toward the shore, and I checked to make sure my bathing suit was in place and followed him to the blanket. There sat another platter on ice, with a mound of fresh and exotic fruits and a bottle of champagne with two glasses. I grabbed a towel from my bag and dried off. I offered it to Rafael, and he just wrapped it around his waist and sat down on the blanket. He opened the bottle and poured it in both flutes. I sat facing him on the blanket and watched him. He handed one to me, and when I touched his hand reaching for the glass, he just stared at me and we both held the glass. It seemed like minutes had passed before he let go. His touch was irresistible. I looked up to him and he was smiling. I shook my head, as if I could remove the thoughts that crowded it.

"Are you okay?" He asked me.

"Are you?" I asked thinking that he must be dying for release.

"I am more than just okay. Feeling your pleasure was more rewarding than having my own."

Who says things like that? I felt so overwhelmed with his sexuality and gentleness that I probably could have another orgasm just looking at him. Looking away from him, I said,

"You, the way you touch me…. I don't know what to say."

"Then don't say anything and just enjoy it."

We picked from the platter and drank the whole bottle of champagne. We told each other stories of places we'd been and childhood memories, getting to know each other just a little, nothing too personal. This was perfect, as far as fantasies go. Oh right, I still had a duty to do here. I had to save my sister. That's what I would tell myself until the end of the week. Then, I'd either die having experienced an incredible fantasy come true, or go back to my home with a newfound passion that I'd had all along which was buried under my daily life and the needs of my family. I now realize the importance of passion. Either way, I hoped to keep this desire, in everything I did, for the rest of my life.

"You look tired," he said softly.

"I am. Do you mind if I go upstairs and take a nap?"

"Not at all. Maybe I can finally get some work done!"

I packed all of my things into my bag and Rafael dropped off the platter at the bar on our way back to the elevators. I didn't look at him directly; I still didn't know what to say right now. We rode up to our floor and walked to our own doors. As I was putting in the code to get in, he asked, "Dinner at nine?"

"Sure." I thought I was supposed to seduce him to get what the goons wanted. Even though he didn't have what they wanted, I was still supposed to be seducing him. Instead, he was seducing me, and worse, I liked it.

I rinsed off in the shower and slithered into bed naked, tired, and my erogenous zones on high alert. I couldn't believe what had just happened. I wondered if this was a test, and I was going to fail miserably. Or was it a lesson that would change my life forever?

6
Chapter

A sudden blare jolted me up in bed. I realized my phone was ringing. It was in the living room in my beach bag. Again it read unknown caller. I answered, "Hello." I sat on the couch realizing I was still naked, but wanted Rafael to hear the conversation. I couldn't focus on being embarrassed.

"Do you have the flash drive yet?" the mouthy goon yelled.

"No, I don't have it and I don't know where it is. Maybe you should try getting into his pants so that he'll invite you to his room." I sensed my attitude flaring again.

"You are a real smart ass, you know?"

"Yes, actually my husband tells me that all the time. I like to think I'm more feisty than a smart ass."

"Maybe you need more motivation."

I heard my sister scream my name, and I demanded to talk to her.

"Maya?"

"Yes, I'm here. Are you okay, are they hurting you?"

"No, not yet anyway. They tell me you're not doing your part. What's going on?"

"Don't worry, I'll get what they want, I just need more time. Be strong, okay."

"Okay." The phone disconnected.

What was going on here? I didn't really know anything. What I did know is that my sister was the tougher and stronger of the two of us. I knew from all the torture I had endured over the years because of her antics. She was probably pissing them off, and in turn, they were putting the pressure on me. That sounds more like Shelby. She was named after the car in the early seventies. I wondered why my name came from my father's Native American Indian ancestors, and my sister had the name of a car.

I heard the code being entered at the door panel, and Rafael burst in with rage. He saw me and stopped short of the living room area. I didn't have time to go to the bedroom and get my robe much less stand up. I sat there naked, with this Adonis-like creation staring at me.

"I'm sorry, I didn't mean to just barge in like that; I was just worried."

"It's okay. I wanted to make sure you could hear the call, so I came out here near the microphone." I smiled because he looked nervous and worried, and very tempting.

"Is something wrong?"

"No, it's just that you are so beautiful, stunning, and strong."

"And so are you." I smiled. "Could you trace the call?"

"Yes we did. I have two men heading out there now. They will contact me with any news."

"Good, so I'll see you at nine then?"

"Yes." He turned around after stealing a glimpse of my body one more time and headed to the door.

I heard the door close and I sighed quietly. I went through the bedroom to the bathroom and started filling the tub with hot water. I needed to unwind. I walked back out past the living room to the kitchen and poured a glass of wine. I smiled. He'd already seen me naked, so what did it matter now. I soaked for a long time, thinking about my family and the things that were important to me.

My mother died ten years ago when she lost her fight with breast cancer. I missed her a lot. My father found love again, thanks to Anne-Marie. My mother knew her and liked her. I think she would be happy for my dad. I loved the happiness they give each other. My father had found himself again, and I loved them both very much. I also gained two awesome stepbrothers, and I loved when we were all together.

Then I thought of Matt. What happened to us? I missed the things we used to do, the way we used to be together. The way he used to touch me. I came here unsure of what would become of our marriage; I was hoping to have some time to think. I lingered in the tub until my hands looked like prunes. I looked at my phone and it was only seven thirty. I had plenty of time to go sit on the balcony with my wine and thoughts.

The sky was bright but getting darker earlier, and the sun was close to setting. I waited to see the dimming of the day, and then I started getting ready for dinner. I did my makeup just like I did if I were going out any other evening, smoky eyes in shades of bronzes and browns. I went to the closet for something to wear. I decided on the black leather skirt that went down to my mid-calf and was slit up the left thigh. Black strappy heels and a cream colored, off the shoulder light sweater completed the look. I loved the way it fit me, hugging me just below my shoulders. I was ready and hungry.

I walked out of the bedroom and toward the front door, and Rafael was standing in the hallway when I opened it. He was dressed in black slacks with an ivory shirt unbuttoned at the top. He really looked edible.

"Shall we, Senora?"

"It would be my pleasure, Senor."

He escorted me to the elevators and pushed the button to go down. My arm was hooked around his and we stood silently waiting. When we reached the lobby downstairs, he asked me if I wanted to eat inside or outside on the deck. I said inside and we were shown to a table in the back, very quiet and dark.

"You look beautiful," he said and smiled.

"That's funny, I was thinking the same thing about you! Any news?" I asked him.

"We think your sister is being held at a storage building about five miles from here. My guys are on foot waiting so see if and when anyone comes in or out, before they get close enough to see if she's there. Everything is going to be okay. I promise you that."

He ordered a bottle of Pinot Grigio and we looked at the menus. I always ordered salmon when I ate out. No one else in my house liked it, so I never made it at home.

Dinner was wonderful. We kept the conversation light. Who knew if the things he shared with me about his childhood or family were even true. I still enjoyed his company and the way he made me feel.

Rafael drank what was left of our bottle of wine, had another sent outside to the bar, and then paid the check. We walked outside and sat at a table. There were only four men sitting together at another table, cracking jokes and laughing. The band tonight was more Latin-sounding, and I only knew how to salsa. Matt and I tried to learn the tango for our wedding, but that didn't work out so well. Matt had two left feet.

"Would you like to dance?" Rafael asked me.

"I'd love to."

As soon as I stood up, he took his jacket off and rolled up his sleeves, then put his hand on the small of my back and followed me to the floor. We danced. We danced like they do on television. I was in awe of him, and I was in awe of myself. I hadn't let go of myself like this in years, not caring what someone would say, or who was watching me. I just let go. After a couple of songs and feeling hot in more ways than one, the music slowed down as if the band knew we needed to be closer together. I put one hand on his chest and the other held the back of his neck. He had both arms around my waist, almost touching my butt. He started whispering in Spanish next to my neck. I was fluent in Spanish, but he didn't know that. I knew what he wanted. I understood everything he said, everything he wanted to do to me. He continued breathing and whispering until I couldn't take it anymore. My heart was racing. I grabbed his hand and led him back to our table. I handed him his jacket and took my purse. I started walking inside and to the elevator with Rafael close behind me. The doors opened right away, like they were waiting for us.

I led him to my condo and pushed in the code. The door closed behind us, and we were already kissing with desire and fury. I started unbuttoning his shirt, while his tongue played with mine, tasting me. He went for the zipper on the back of my skirt; it was difficult with my backside pressed against the wall in the entry. I pushed him back against the opposite wall. He grabbed my ass and pulled me into him, kissing my neck with such passion and desire. I got his shirt off and touched his chest; his skin was hot and soft. I rubbed his nipples with the tips of my fingers, and Rafael moaned so loud I felt it through my entire body. I was unbuttoning his pants as my skirt hit the floor. He was incredibly surprised that I didn't have any panties on. I had never felt this kind of lust or pleasure before now. The bulge in his pants felt like it was going to burst out. He was a god, and I was sure I would be using that word a lot that night. I was definitely melting quickly and wanted more. I broke off from his lips and took a step back. While staring into each other's eyes, I lifted my sweater over my head and dropped it on the floor. He unzipped his pants and dropped them to the floor. Never breaking eye contact, I leaned down and removed my shoes. He took off his briefs along with his shoes and socks. We stood looking at each other, naked in the hallway. I stepped close to him and he put his hands around my waist and lifted me off the floor. I wrapped my legs around him and sucked on his lips, licked them and grazed my teeth against them. They were full and luscious just like the rest of him. He was walking in the direction of the bedroom and I could barely contain myself. He lay me down on the edge of my bed and never lost his position. His lips slowed, becoming more sensual, and when I felt him relax just a little, I rolled him over so that I was on top. He smiled at me, and I started kissing his neck while I introduced our sexes. I rubbed myself over his huge erection. I was so wet.

Just then his phone rang back in his pants pocket near the entry. We both groaned, and he got up to retrieve his pants.

"This better be life or death." He answered his phone, turned to look at me, and said, "Give me a minute, I'll be right there." Rafael disconnected the call and looked down.

"What is it?"

Chapter 7

"They have a visual on your sister. She's in a storage unit, sitting on a couch watching television. There is no one else inside the unit, only one guy at the door outside."

"What are we going to do?"

"My team and I will get her back as soon as we find where the other hired guns are."

"Why do we have to wait? Why can't we just go get her?"

"I need to meet with my team and find out what we know."

"Okay."

He gathered his clothes from the entry and dressed. Rafael came back to me and kissed me differently; it was like longing mixed with regret. I'm sure he was feeling the same disappointment I was right now. He walked out the door and made sure it locked behind him. I stood in the entry and really couldn't believe how alone I felt. I picked up all the clothes and my shoes and took them to the bedroom. I slipped into my robe and went to the kitchen, poured a glass of wine, and sat outside on the balcony. I smoked a cigarette to calm my nerves, and just enjoyed the evening breeze from the water. I didn't hear from Rafael that night. I didn't know if he was coming back or not.

I couldn't believe what almost happened. I was feeling sensations and emotions that I hadn't felt in so long. I wanted Rafael. But what I needed was my husband to want me the way Rafael did. I wasn't really sure what or how to feel about Rafael, Matt, and my sister. The only thing I did know was that I missed Hayden so much; I wished I could just kiss and hug him right then. I was tired enough from the day's excitement to go to bed, so I did.

When I woke up, it was bright in the room and the sun was already over the west side of the building. It was afternoon I was sure. I went to get my cell phone to see what time it was. It was one twenty in the afternoon. I couldn't believe I slept that long, but I had no idea what time it was when I went to bed. I hadn't slept like that in years. I knew I came here to relax, sleep and have fun, but relaxing was the most difficult part right now. With this whole hostage situation and having a fantasy almost come true, my emotions and my body were tied up in knots.

I started some coffee and went to shower. After drying off, I put my robe on and went to get my coffee. Rafael was standing in the kitchen holding out a mug to me. I smiled. It was good to see him. He looked very tired, but happy and smiling.

"Hi," I said but wasn't surprised to see him.

"Buenos dias."

"Did you get any sleep?"

"Some."

"Any news?"

"We worked all night and found the men that came to your condo are renting a condo two floors up. They have been watching your every move. We have a plan to take them all down, but we have to find who hired them or who they are working with first."

"Did you see my sister?"

"Yes."

"Do you think she has anything to do with this?"

"No."

"What do we do now?"

"We stay relaxed and wait."

"Wait for what?"

"All the information on these men holding your sister, and the buyer they had lined up."

I started wanting to know what this whole thing was all about. I wondered what was on this mysterious flash drive, why it had to be stolen and turned over to the CIA, and why the goons wanted it so bad.

"What is on the flash drive?" I flat out asked him.

"Times and shipments dates of guns and ammo that we send overseas to freedom fighters in oppressed nations. If they were to intercept these shipments, we could lose a lot more than the artillery. There are also names and information of agents in deep undercover that we have in other countries. We can't afford for anyone else to have this information." He didn't tell me too much.

"Who are these people, the Spanish mafia?" I said joking, but also knowing it was possible.

"Something like that." Rafael stated.

"Why do the goons want it so bad?"

"They had a buyer set up and ready to purchase the information. When the file was copied by a rogue agent, the file was deleted and the only copy of it was on the flash drive."

"Well that assures me that my sister isn't involved!"

My sister was smart but she couldn't possibly have anything to do with this mess.

I felt unusually calm. We went out to the table on the balcony and drank our coffee.

"What are we going to do with the rest of today?" I asked, knowing it was probably around two o'clock in the afternoon by now. I went inside to turn the television on. It just happened to be Nickelodeon, Hayden's favorite channel. It was always what we watched at home. I was really missing him right now and wished that I could talk to him.

I still hadn't gone to the store, so I couldn't make breakfast, although it was after lunch time when I thought about it.

"Are you hungry?" I asked. Rafael was still sitting on the balcony. He walked inside and to the kitchen where I was standing.

"Starving," he said taking me in his arms and kissing me so passionately I didn't feel hungry for food anymore. I was hungry for him. I heard a light tap on the door. He went to the door and it was a platter of sandwiches and chips.

"How did you…." I was confused, and he was always three steps ahead.

"My team heard you. They must like you; they never do things like this without my asking."

"Oh my god." I covered my mouth, feeling a little embarrassed. "Did they hear us last night in the entry?" I went from understanding his explanation of the food to wondering if they heard every moan and groan from our short lived passion the night before. Not to mention they could have seen the whole thing on the cameras. That's why they liked me; I gave them a very entertaining show to watch last night. Oh God. I should make them popcorn next time. If there is a next time.

"Some of it." He smirked

"Do you want to go to the boardwalk; there are a lot of stores and coffee shops down there?"

"I'm sorry but we have to stay here so I can be in contact with my team in case anything happens. I need to be ready."

I looked down at my toes. They looked really good in the sheer color I painted them; it made my skin look darker.

"Maya, I am so sorry. I promise you this, when we have your sister back and the hired guns out of commission, you can do anything you want to do for the rest of your vacation. I will see to it myself that you get to do everything you came here to do."

"So then we eat our sandwiches and watch cartoons," I said and picked up the tray of sandwiches. We went over to the couch and sat with our little buffet. He was getting a kick out of Sponge Bob. It was the first time I heard him laugh. Even that was sexy. We had several beers sent up in an ice bucket and went to sit outside on the balcony. He smoked with me like someone who only smoked socially. I was enjoying this time with him. He was amazing at telling stories, even if it was hard to listen past his accent. I was adjusting to how he made me weak in the knees, but stronger as a woman, at the same time.

We came inside and lay on the couch, his arms around me and my head resting on his shoulder. I guessed we must have fallen asleep because when his phone rang, we were both startled. We sat next to each other on the couch while he listened to the person on the phone talk. I knew something was wrong when he put his head in his hand and was rubbing his forehead. He hung up and then used both hands to rub his head.

"What is it?" I was worried.

"It looks like they are going to move your sister. All we can do now is watch and see where they take her, and maybe it will give us some more information."

"Please don't lose her." I had to keep telling myself that they knew what they were doing. "Do you have to go?"

"Yes, but if I can, I'll come back later tonight, if you want me to." His face was asking.

"I'd really like that."

"Thank you for sharing so much of yourself with me this afternoon. I really enjoyed it and hopefully we can continue later." He kissed me and walked out.

8
Chapter

Just in time to go outside and watch the sunset. I went out on the balcony and had a cigarette. I loved the sunset, but my favorite time of the day was when I got up in the morning before anyone else, took my coffee out on the back porch, and watched the sun come up. I'd always needed that little bit of peace to start my day. I didn't always get the time to do things for myself, between taking care of Hayden, the house, and the yard. "When I get home I'm just going to have to make time for myself." I thought. "Something else will just have to go undone."

It was Sunday night. I went into the living room and turned on the television. I had missed all my favorite shows last week getting everyone ready for their trips. Now I could sit back and watch them all at once with no commercials or interruptions with the on demand channel. This was great!

When I had enough of the television, I went for a nice hot bath. I poured in my favorite jasmine bubble bath and lit all the candles around the tub. The water was steaming, but when I sat down, I felt my entire body collapse. I had a towel as a pillow and was so relaxed I probably could have gone to sleep. Then I heard something in the kitchen. Before I could even sit up, I saw Rafael was standing in the doorway to the bathroom with a plate of chocolate-covered strawberries and a bottle of champagne with two flutes. I started to giggle because that's all he had. No clothes, holding a tray, just standing there naked.

"Strawberry?" He smiled and walked toward the tub.

"Only if you join me and feed them to me." I smiled, wondering where my boldness was coming from.

He put the tray down and stepped in. The tub was huge and he was only about six feet tall, but he sat facing me and I put my legs over his so he could stretch out. He leaned in and put a strawberry to my lips. I licked the chocolate, then sucked on the rest before I took it in my mouth. It was delicious, but it didn't come close to how delicious Rafael looked right now. I reached past him to get another strawberry and fed it to him. He took one bite and pulled me onto his lap and shared his bite with me. Our tongues played with the fruit, tasting it, passing it back and forth in our mouths until it was gone. The kissing went on and I felt his erection hard underneath me. We relaxed a little; things were getting a little too hot, too fast. We sipped on the champagne in between washing each other and touching each other. There wasn't much conversation, but I didn't need to talk right now. I needed him. I needed to feel how he was making me feel.

We finished the bottle and were laughing at everything. I didn't know if he felt as giddy as I did, but we were making each other laugh so hard. He told me a story from one of his missions and how he had a little girl walk in on him while he was showering in a safe house. I could only imagine the look on her face, seeing Rafael naked and wondering what was going through her mind.

I told him about my son and how he had become a breast man. Kids are so funny saying whatever comes to mind. Hayden had asked me one day,

"Mom, what are those?" as he used one of his fingers to poke my breast. I explained to him that they were girl parts and that I called them boobs. He responded,

"I like boobs."

My face was starting to hurt from laughing so hard.

Rafael gave me a very coy look when we stopped laughing, and I knew it was time to get out of the bath. He stepped out first and turned around reaching out his hand to help me out of the tub, but as soon as I stood up, he was leaning over the tub to sweep me up in his arms. He placed me on the counter and pushed himself between my legs. Between the hot bath and the touch of his skin, I was on fire. His hands were holding my back, covering it with his heat. Devouring kisses moved from my mouth to my neck, and he started whispering against my skin in Spanish. It was hard to concentrate, but I understood every word. He said,

"Quiero cojerte tan duro que nunca olvidaras, porque yo nunca te olvido," which translates in English to, "I want to fuck you so hard that you will never forget me, because I will never forget you."

He picked me up by my ass and almost slammed me up against the wall behind us. He was literally holding me up with one arm across my butt and the other holding up the wall. We were still soaking wet and full of bubbles. He rubbed his erection up and down over my sex and growled like a bear. I had never before heard the absolute desire and passion I heard in his voice and moans. I was being pretty quiet because all of my senses were busy. I was enjoying his passion right now, the way he was tender but strong in his desire. I was slipping down the wall and one leg fell to the floor. He grabbed my other leg before it had a chance to follow, and he pulled it high around his waist. With one very hard thrust, he was inside me, consuming me. He stayed very still and then another thrust, and he was all the way inside me as far and deep as he could go. He was kissing me so hard but soft at the same time, gentle but hungry. To hold myself in this place, I was holding one of his shoulders and the back of his neck so tightly.

While never leaving his place deep inside me, he picked me up off of the wall, water and bubbles flying everywhere. He took me to the bed and lay me down, pulling himself all the way out and then all the way inside. It was magnificent, the constant jolts of excitement that passed between us, like electricity. I rolled him over so that I was on top of him and felt him deeper inside me than before. I couldn't hold back any longer and started a cry of my own. He rolled me over and under him again, and within a minute he was climaxing with me. He kept moving and breathing against my neck, and I was still feeling the rippling of my own climax. He didn't stop. He started licking my nipples and flicking them with his tongue, sucking them until they stood up high and swollen. I felt his heat shooting into me, and I was coming again or still feeling aftershocks, I wasn't even sure. My eyes were locked in on his and his on mine. Rafael lowered himself closer to me. I felt his breath on my mouth and he kissed me, teasing my mouth with his, slowing down and relaxing. Easing out of the clenching moment, he fell next to me and ran his fingers from my neck to my belly button. That alone was shocking to my senses right then. I felt so sensitive. My skin was so hot and I thought I could pass out at any moment. I didn't want to miss a second of this experience. He made love to me until the sun came up. It was like he wanted my body and my heart to remember him, never really talking, just touching and feeling each other, and sharing our passion. I was so tired, we curled up watching the light of daybreak reflect on the water and finally fell asleep.

Chapter 9

We woke up starving. I didn't think I'd ever burned that many calories at one time. He kissed me and I could still taste the champagne and strawberries.

"Would you like breakfast, lunch or dinner?" I asked him, not knowing what time it was. He just lay there watching me as I rolled out of bed and put my robe on.

"Breakfast." Rafael moaned like he would rather stay where he was in bed than to get up, even to eat.

I walked into the kitchen and started the coffee, went to the phone and ordered everything from the hotel restaurant breakfast menu. I picked up his clothes that left a trail from the front door though the kitchen and ended in the living room. I laughed to myself and I brought them to the bedroom and set them on the bed. I heard the shower and went in to join him. I took my robe off and stepped in. The water was warm and relaxing against my body, aching from the night we shared. He grabbed me around the waist and pulled me directly under the shower head with him, kissing me and stroking my body, sending me into another state of complete bliss.

We washed our hair and lathered each other with my body wash, but before things could get any hotter, I said,

"Our breakfast should be here any minute."

He sighed with disappointment and smiled at me, then turned the water off.

As soon as we stepped out of the shower, there was a knock at the door. He grabbed a towel, wrapped it around his waist, and went to answer the door. The waiter brought in a buffet on wheels. I waited until he left and came out wearing only Rafael's shirt. It was huge on me and covered everything. It smelled like him. It felt so incredibly sexy feeling my naked body brush against the soft material of his shirt. He went to the bedroom and came out with his boxer briefs on that looked like they were made for him, like a second skin, tight and showing the definition of his sensational ass and thighs. We took the many platters of food out to the balcony, and I brought out the pot of coffee and two cups. We sat and realized we would never eat all this food. Rafael looked at me and said,

"You ordered enough food for twenty people." He laughed.

"I didn't know what you liked so I ordered everything they had." I felt hungry enough to eat everything on the table.

"Last night… I just want to tell you it was the most amazing night of my life. You are incredible." He smiled and took my hand in his and brought it up to his lips and kissed it. He held my hand for a few moments and I felt like I needed to say something too.

"You are quite amazing yourself! You showed me that I still have passion. You reminded me that I am not just a mom and a wife, but a woman." I got up and kissed him.

"Now what do you say about inviting your team for breakfast?" I smiled not caring what we were wearing or the condition of our emotions. I didn't really know how he was feeling, but my emotions felt like a hurricane inside my head. I wanted to laugh and cry at the same time. I was beside myself with the things that had happened between Rafael and me. I felt alive and beautiful, but I was full of regret and remorse. I was unsure how to handle my feelings and ended up doing what I usually do, and put them aside for now.

Within two minutes, Rafael's team let themselves into my condo, and each of them found a seat with us, outside around the table on the large balcony. Rafael introduced me to the four of them. First was Rock. He only nodded his head to me, and then poured himself a cup of coffee. He looked like a body builder. His hair was dark and cut like he was in the military. He seemed quiet and conservative. Next was Kit, who I recognized from the beach when she brought us a couple of drinks. She hugged me and sat back down. She was shorter than me, maybe five foot two and in great physical shape. Her hair was blond, cut into a short bob, and she tucked it behind her ears. She was fair skinned and had the most brilliant blue eyes I had ever seen. Then Tex, who reached for my hand and kissed it, but not without a look from Rafael. He seemed very gentlemanly. He wore a cowboy hat, jeans and boots. He had longer light brown hair, green eyes, and a five o'clock shadow that looked sexy on him. He winked at me and then sat down. Then finally Techno, who shyly said that it was nice to meet me. He looked like an average man, no significant physical or personality traits, the boy next door would describe him best. He was very quiet and bashful. I felt like we were all friends even though we had not met before now. As soon as they all had food piled on their plates and everyone had coffee, they started discussing the situation with the hired guns and my sister. They all were speaking Spanish, so I wouldn't understand. I got most of what they were saying but I asked,

"What's going on?"

"We have your sister in view and she's fine. They moved her to another warehouse a few miles away. We've made contact with the potential buyers saying we had the flash drive and they would need to deal with us directly. We are going in to get your sister tonight before the hired guns figure out what is going on. She'll be home safely tonight."

"Thank you." I knew I trusted him before, but now I felt sure Shelby would be okay.

We ate almost everything, talking about what a vacation they were all having. They were supposed to be enjoying this time off work, and I was supposed to be enjoying some time alone. I thought this could all be part of a bigger lesson for me. I just hadn't figured it out yet.

Rafael loaded all the platters and plates back on the rolling table and pushed it outside the door. His team thanked us for breakfast and returned next door, saying that they would see Rafael later. He sat down in the leather recliner and I sat on his lap facing him. I didn't have any underwear on so I felt his bulge strengthen and grow harder with every kiss I gave him. I tickled his neck with my tongue and licked behind his ears. I felt myself getting wet from the friction of him against me. I reached under my legs and tugged at the elastic of his boxer briefs and managed to pull them down far enough to expose his erection. I rubbed myself against him for just a few moments before he found my wet spot, and I slowly lowered myself onto him. We moaned at the same time, feeling each other. We started kissing and he could feel me getting close by the intensity in my kisses. Rafael started licking my ear and his breathing was getting harder along with his erection inside me. I leaned back and put my hands behind me on his knees and arched my back as I started to climax. He was playing with my breasts, feeling them and pinching my nipples. Then I could feel him tensing up and the veins in his neck bulging out as he grabbed my waist and his head tilted upwards. He moaned my name, holding me so tightly, then I could feel him letting go. I slowed down my movements until we both felt the other relaxing our muscles. I just sat on him enjoying his mouth and the pleasure in it. I rested my head against his chest and said,

"Can you handle a few more days of me, you, and phenomenal sex?" I said knowing that what we had was more than just great sex.

"I can't think of anywhere else I would rather be."

"Do you need to go get some work done with your team?"

"In a minute."

"Do you think they just watched us?" I thought to myself that even if they weren't watching, it felt alluring knowing they could be.

"No."

I wondered if they knew him so well as to give him privacy when he needed it. If aiding rebels, near-death experiences, kidnappings, and traveling for weeks on end didn't make a team airtight close, then I didn't know what would.

I stood up and unbuttoned his shirt and laid it on the back of one of the dining room chairs knowing he had to go, but teasing him with undressing and walking away made me feel empowered. I went and got a soapy towel and washed him off, then went back into the bathroom and cleaned myself. When I returned to the living room in my robe, he was dressed and ready to go. I knew he had to go, I wasn't sad. I was ready for some down time anyway. I was in the middle of a very good book, and since I was up to date on my shows, it seemed like a prime reading opportunity. Rafael kissed me and held me close until he had to say goodbye for now.

I went to grab some pillows from the bed and found a comfy spot on the couch. I started thinking of all the things that had happened in the last three days. No one would believe me if I told this story, not that I planned to, but my three older nephews would love to hear about this. At seventeen, eighteen, and nineteen, they loved the excitement of life. I loved them like my own, but I also had unique friendships with each of them. I didn't even think they would believe this story. I started thinking about them and the things they were going through right now with their parents getting divorced. I had always been so proud of how strong they were and thankful that they had been so involved in the youth group at their church. It had given them strength and faith, something that they really needed right now.

It was a shame that almost all of our friends were either getting divorced, unhappily married, or separating. The couples that seemed happy were already divorced and had re-married or were newly married and still in the honeymoon phase. It didn't say a lot for the institution of marriage.

10
Chapter

I must have dosed off because the next thing I knew, Rafael was touching my face trying to wake me up, and when I opened my eyes he asked,

"What were you dreaming about? You were smiling in your sleep."

"My son. What's going on? Is everything okay?"

"We are going to get your sister now."

"Okay, just let me get dressed," I said and quickly stood up.

"No, I can't let you go." Rafael was vigorously shaking his head.

"If you leave me here alone, I'm a sitting duck. You said the other goons are here. What am I supposed to do?"

"Okay, but promise you'll stay in the car." He looked at me and put his hands on my shoulders like he was dead serious.

He left to go get what he needed and I got dressed. Jeans, a sweater, and some sneakers, a little gloss on my lips. Worked for me. I was starting to feel scared and anxious.

He came back to get me and had a shoulder holster with a gun. His tight, black, long sleeve shirt he had on showed the definition in his chest and shoulders. With a gun strapped to him, looking hot and dangerous, I didn't know if I could control my attraction. But we certainly didn't have time for fooling around now.

We went downstairs to the entrance and his team was already waiting. We hopped into the black SUV, so typical for the CIA, and pulled away. They were discussing their plans of who was taking each entrance on every side of the building, and I just sat quietly and listened until we reached the street along the side of the warehouse. It was a very large two story metal building with a fence around most of the property. They all hopped out and Rafael told me to stay in the car. Like hell! There was no way I was just going to sit there. My fear held me back for a moment, and I contemplated staying in the car. I wanted to get my sister back and see that she was alright. I couldn't wait any longer. I watched to see where they were headed and then followed them a few minutes later. I ran along the outside of the building and stayed close to the wall. I reached the back of the warehouse and peeked around the corner. I saw the quiet goon that came to my condo the first two times walking toward me. I stood flat against the wall until I could hear him getting close to the corner. As soon as I saw his foot, I held my arm straight, and with all my might, hit him in the Adam's apple with the side of my hand like some karate move. "Wow, I'm stronger than I thought," I said out loud. It gagged him so hard he fell backwards and to the ground. I once read a magazine article titled "21 Ways to Kill a Man with Your Bare Hands." I was happy to see that at least one worked. Not that I wanted to kill him, but I was flying by the seat of my pants here. He took labored breaths and lay there. I couldn't believe I just did that. I walked around the corner to the back side of the building and took a closer look at the man now on the ground.

"Dios Mio, I could have killed you. Why didn't you stay in the car?" said a startled voice.

I looked up from the body and saw Rafael with his gun drawn in my direction.

"I don't like to be told what to do; besides it's my sister."

Rafael shot me a furious look and shook his head.

"Nice work, where did you learn to do that?"

"I read a lot."

Rafael leaned down to check the man's pulse. He rolled the guy over and put handcuffs on him. When I looked up, I saw another goon, one I hadn't had the pleasure of meeting yet. He was just an arm's length away from me, so when he put his arms up to grab me, I grabbed for the insides of his arms and kneed him in the balls, hard. He was on the ground hunched over, so I elbowed him behind the neck and he was out cold. I turned around to see Rafael with his gun drawn again. He put it back in the holster and used zip ties to bind the second man in place. He wasn't going anywhere either.

"I am supposed to be protecting you, in case you forgot. Remind me to never get on your bad side."

We drug the two tied up goons inside the closest door on the back side of the warehouse and left them there in the small storage unit. We found another door about twenty-five feet away and went inside where my sister was being comforted by Kit and Tex. She was safe! I began to cry as I ran and hugged her. She wasn't crying or upset at all.

"Are you okay?" I held her back to look at her.

"I'm fine. I just want to go home."

Rafael informed me they had a helicopter waiting to take her home. Rafael and Rock started asking her questions about the men who took her and how. She didn't know any of their names but described them perfectly and identified several of the men from photos Rafael showed her. When she had answered all their questions and explained that she had gotten a phone call from a man saying he had me, she met them where she was told to go. They put her in the trunk for the drive to north Florida and found the first warehouse they arrived at. I was happy to hear that they didn't hurt her, but they had made several threats. We all walked back to the SUV and Rafael started boasting to his team what I had done. I was barely paying attention to their comments; I was just sitting there looking at my sister and holding her hand. She was fine and such a strong person.

We drove to the open field where the chopper was waiting, and I hugged her goodbye.

"Are you going to be okay?" I asked in a concerned way.

"Yeah, I just want to get home. How about you, are you okay?"

"I'm fine. I guess I'll see you at the next family gathering."

She nodded and walked away. As they lifted off the ground she waved her hand.

I walked back to the SUV and got in. Rafael and his team were all looking at me.

"What did I do now?" I asked with my usual attitude.

They just chuckled a little and continued their conversation in Spanish, like I didn't understand what they were saying. But then they still didn't know I spoke Spanish. They really underestimated the stay-at-home mom.

We reached the condo complex and parked in the parking garage. Everyone was quiet as we walked to the elevators. The rush had clearly worn off for me. I was so relieved that Shelby was on her way home.

"Now what?" I asked as if I didn't hear their conversation in the car.

"We sent medics for the four hired guns at the warehouse. There are still two in the building here; we have agents on their way to take them into custody. It's over now.

I kept my promise this far. My team is leaving tomorrow, but I can stay for the rest of the week if you want me to."

"Can you handle me for the rest of the week?" I smiled the way he smiled at me and felt this overwhelming feeling of freedom. I hadn't done a lot of the things I planned to do this week, but inside I felt accomplished. I felt happy and wanted to enjoy my new friends. I'd never really had many close friends other than a few couples that we knew and would get together with on occasion, and my scrapbooking group.

"How about we all have dinner together tonight?" I asked.

"Sounds good to us!" Tex replied and the others nodded in agreement.

"Great, I'll meet you all downstairs at nine."

I went into my condo and took a quick shower; I only had an hour to get ready. My make-up always took the longest, my hair was easy. It is bone straight so I just took the flat iron to it and flipped out some of the layers. I picked out a black dress that had pearl buttons down the left side, and the bottom was slit up the same leg to the end of the pearls. A pearl choker and earrings I had made several years ago, but had never worn them until now, I slid on my black heels and grabbed my purse. I checked the time on my phone and I still had fifteen minutes. I walked out of the bedroom and saw Rafael standing in the kitchen.

"Hi, I was just going to have a cigarette before I left. Would you like to join me?" I smiled at him. He looked divine in a pair of black pants and a white button-down shirt.

"I'd love to, and may I say that your beauty is only matched by your ferocity."

He always knew what to say and left me feeling wonderful about myself, something I hadn't felt in so long. There was always something more important that came before my needs. I thought it was just part of being a wife and mother. I was wrong. I needed to feel like a woman again, and this was certainly working.

"Thank you, Senor. You look extremely stunning yourself."

Ten minutes later we were taking the elevators down to the restaurant. I felt so excited and anxious at the same time. I couldn't take my eyes off of him. We met his team and we all sat together at a large circular table.

Dinner was so much fun. Who knew that CIA agents could actually let loose and be so entertaining. They were telling stories and dirty jokes, and Techno even fell out of his chair he was laughing so hard. After we finished our two-hour meal, we all went outside to the tiki bar. We put a couple of small tables together to accommodate all of us and placed our drink orders. We laughed so hard and had such a great time dancing, talking and getting to know each other. I was sad when the night came to an end. They all hugged me and thanked me for the evening.

Rafael kissed me. I was exhausted by now; the adrenaline rush had clearly worn off. I just wanted to get some sleep. We all went upstairs, and Rafael and his team went to their own door and I went to mine.

"Get some rest," I said in their direction. "Thanks to all of you for helping me get my sister. It was nice to meet you. Stay safe."

They all just smiled and went inside.

I let myself in my condo and pushed the door closed until it locked. I stood leaning against the door for several minutes just thinking of the things that had happened today. I went into the bedroom, changed my clothes and went out the French doors leading from the bedroom to the balcony and had a cigarette. I smoked a little of my hand rolled cigarette and sat outside for quite a while, just quiet, not thinking about anything, just clearing my head, emptying all my thoughts. There was still some beer left over that I had put in the refrigerator. I stepped inside the sliding doors to the living room, and there were two men sitting on the couch. It must have been the two goons that were still in the building, I assumed, because I had never seen them before.

"What now?" I said as they stared at me. I knew that Rafael would see them here and bust down the door at any moment.

"It seems you haven't been behaving yourself."

"The pot is legal, it's not real, and I bought it at a convenience store," I said like I didn't know what they were talking about.

"It seems you didn't take our warnings seriously."

I didn't know what to say; usually the smart remarks came naturally. Ask anyone on my husband's side of the family.

Did they know my sister was free? Maybe they had no idea what had happened and were trying to threaten me. I wasn't sure. But I was starting to wonder where Rafael was. I thought he would have been here by now.

"I'm doing the best I can. I haven't found the flash drive and he is leaving tonight."

"Don't act stupid with us." He walked toward me and stood close to my face.

"What are you talking about?"

"We already know about your sister, and now it seems your friend has tried to take over some of our business. We don't like when things like this happen."

I went and sat on the couch like I didn't know anything about what was going on. It also occurred to me that if Rafael's team was leaving tomorrow, they might have disconnected all their cameras and microphones and were packing up right now, having some debriefing, or something.

What did I know about how they handled these things? One of them walked over to me and backhanded me in the mouth. I didn't see that coming. The pain was instant and sharp, and when I touched my lips they were bleeding.

"What do you want me to do now?" I yelled at him.

"You are going to tell us what your boyfriends plans are so we can get what we came here for."

"I don't know anything." I wanted to tell them that there was no flash drive and it was in the hands of the government, but then they wouldn't need me anymore. The thought of being killed as a consequence held me back from saying anything at all.

"Then I guess we will just be keeping you company until your friend comes to us."

"He has already left. We said goodbye after dinner tonight."

"We know that he hasn't left yet. For your sake you better hope he hasn't and comes to give you one more goodbye kiss." He smirked at me, and then smacked me again, but this time right across the cheek. This wasn't the first time I'd been hit by a man. Having gone through many abusive relationships in my life, I knew how to handle the hitting, but my temper would come out in return. Only this time it could get me killed. At this point, my only recourse was to remain calm.

If I thought the other two goons were dumb and dumber, this pair would be rude and ruder. As big as the other two, but ugly faces with scars and tattoos around their necks like they were in some gang. There was certainly no need to hit me. Now what was I going to do? I knew that Rafael would come to see me sooner rather than later, and I refused to cry. Emboldened by the success at the warehouse, I was thinking about how I could take them both out and get out of here. They had guns; my biggest weapon was going to be myself or one of the dull kitchen knives that came with the condo. I needed to think so I sat quietly and ignored the questions. Then "whack" another slap across the face, and another. Still, I remained quiet. The larger of the two, not by much, hit me several more times for not answering his questions, and I was starting to get my attitude back. Just then I heard a knock at the door. I froze; if it were Rafael, he would have just used the code.

"Go answer it. Unless it's the agent, send them away."

I walked to the door. The two men had their guns drawn, pointing them at me.

"Who is it?"

"Your appetizers and wine."

It was Kit, the only woman on Rafael's team. I felt relieved. If anyone saw her, they would just think that she worked here.

I turned around to the two men and explained that I had ordered some finger food and a bottle of wine before I left the bar. They nodded and I opened the door.

"Thank you," I said as I looked at her. She saw my lip, and until then I had forgotten it was still bloody. Her expression went serious.

"You're welcome. If there is anything else just call."

I took the tray and closed the door. I brought it to the living room and put it on the coffee table. My plans for the evening were not going well. Kit must have wanted to see what was going on. Maybe they heard something next door.

"Help yourselves. I wasn't expecting company or I would have ordered more."

They did help themselves, and I took the bottle of wine to the kitchen to get a glass. I saw a flash on the balcony. Rafael was swinging over from the next balcony; I had to do something, make a distraction so that they wouldn't see him.

"Do you want something to drink?" I asked them so that they would turn around to me in the kitchen. One of them walked toward me and said,

"I'll get that."

"I can get it myself." I took the wine opener out of the drawer, and as he got closer to me, I dropped the bottle opener to the floor. I bent down to pick it up and jabbed him in the thigh with the corkscrew and he fell to his knees on the floor.

Just then Rafael came in from outside and pistol whipped the other guy in the temple, sending him straight to the floor. I heard the code at the door and the others came in from next door with guns out. They came around the corner and saw me standing next to the guy I stabbed. He tried to grab me and I kicked him right where I stabbed him in the leg, and he fell sideways on the floor. Rock handcuffed him as Rafael did the same with the unconscious one. Rafael walked into the kitchen and gave me a good look over and asked,

"Are you okay? What happened?"

"I'm fine. They came in pissed about you stealing business from them and were trying to rough me up to get information. I told them that you all left already, but he didn't believe me. They obviously still have people watching. I thought there were agents coming to take these men into custody." I started to get tears in my eyes, and when I looked at Rafael, he reached for me and pulled me into him. The two goons were moved to Rafael's room and his team left us alone. He held me for a few minutes and then led me to the couch.

"Sit down. Let me get you some ice for your face and lip."

"I'm fine, really."

"Humor me. If you don't do something about the swelling now, it's only going to get worse."

I nodded my head, which was starting to pound, and went to the bathroom to take a look and wash my face. It wasn't that bad. My lip was swollen but not bleeding anymore. I returned to the couch and Rafael brought me a bag of ice wrapped in a towel along with a glass of wine. We sat and talked and I told him everything that had happened. He got up and went to the phone, dialed, and was talking to someone when I went out on the balcony to have a cigarette. I could hear him talking in Spanish and his tone was stern, but I didn't hear what he was saying. When I came in, Rafael hung up the phone and sat with me on the couch again.

"Is everything alright?" I was concerned by his body language. He seemed different, nervous or something, I wasn't sure but I had never seen Rafael look this way.

"Yes, it's finally over and your sister and family are safe. It's really over."

"Then what's wrong?"

"All this time we have been protecting and watching several people, and I couldn't protect you when you were right next to me."

"You saved me. In more ways than you know. I knew you would come in and rescue me." I smiled because he looked mad at himself. He needed to know that I was okay and could protect myself. I was a mom, a natural protector. Nothing would have stopped me from leaving here and returning home to my son. Nothing.

"All I want now is to enjoy the rest of my vacation, and I'm hoping you can stay with me for the next few days."

"I made you a promise. What can I do for you now?"

"Will you stay with me tonight?"

"Yes."

"Thank you."

We went to my bed and just held each other. I snuggled against him and rested my head on his chest. His breathing and heartbeat were calming. We both were exhausted, because we were asleep within minutes.

II
Chapter

We woke up early. The sun wasn't even up yet. Rafael was looking at me so sweetly, I wondered if I had been talking in my sleep and said something I shouldn't have. I had to ask.

"What are you smiling at?"

"You." He raised himself up to face me. "Tell me about your family."

"What?"

"I want to know about your husband and son."

"Why?"

"I want to know what it's like through your eyes, having a family."

"Well, my husband's name is Matt; we've been married for almost seven years. Hayden, my son, is four. They're both a handful, and I stay at home and take care of them. I also take care of the lawn, pool, laundry, cooking, cleaning, laundry, picking up boy toys all day, making phone calls, and did I mention more laundry?"

He laughed, and I realized how crazy I must sound to a special ops agent who travels the world and endangers his life every day. I laughed too, and his smile had a special place in my heart. It would always be there. I went on telling him stories about my family, and suddenly I realized we were both learning something about ourselves during this unbelievable journey. It made me think of Matt and our journey right now. I was just unsure of where we were headed if things didn't change. I loved him, but wasn't sure that I was in love with him anymore. I would think sometimes that our relationship seemed more like we were roommates. We just seemed to be arguing about the stupidest things lately, and I think we needed this week away from each other to see that the little things didn't matter as long as we had each other. I just wasn't sure that love was enough. He used to be my best friend.

Hayden was my angel. He was a miracle. I had a terrible pregnancy, scaring me to death for nine months. The doctors took him early because of my blood pressure, and we all agreed to tie my tubes at the same time. It wasn't safe for me or another baby if I were to conceive again. Hayden was perfect and had been a pure joy since the day he was born, on my thirty fifth birthday. I told Rafael all about Hayden. I felt happy sharing my life story with him.

"Anything else you want to know?" I asked.

"What would you like for breakfast?"

"You pick this time."

Rafael called downstairs to the restaurant and ordered, started the coffee brewing, and came back to the bedroom.

"So what would you like to do today?" he asked me as he climbed back into bed.

"I want to go shopping, walk down the boardwalk, and eat lunch somewhere other than here."

He started kissing me and I felt I was in a different life. I wondered if I just woke up in someone else's life. Today was definitely going to be different from my life at home. We must have lost track of time because the knock at the door startled us both. He grabbed his gun from the kitchen before walking to the door. I didn't even know it was in there. I wondered why he was still being protective. I thought that it was all over. He opened the door and it was our breakfast. He pushed his gun in the back of his pants and wheeled the cart in. The door closed and he didn't say anything to the waiter or waitress. Something didn't feel right. I couldn't put my finger on it, just a gut feeling. He brought the table on wheels to the dining room and put all the trays on the table and pushed the cart to the entry hall out of the way. I changed into my robe and sat at the dining table. Rafael brought over the pot of coffee and two cups. We both had biscuits and gravy, fresh fruits, and orange juice. I wondered how he knew that my favorite thing in the world for breakfast, or anytime for that matter, was sausage gravy and biscuits.

"So tell me about your family," I said before taking a sip of my coffee.

"There's nothing to tell really. My mother died when I was seventeen, so I went into the military after I graduated. I made it into the Navy Seals, and from there I went into the CIA. That's all I have."

"I'm sorry about your mom. I lost mine ten years ago and I still miss her. So you're married to your job too, huh?"

"Yes."

"Well you have the rest of your life ahead of you. You can do whatever you want to. Do want to have a family?"

"I've never given it much thought until these last few days." Something had changed in his eyes, but I wasn't sure what it was. Then he said, "Shh."

I just sat there for a moment, and then I heard it too. There was a quiet ticking noise. Rafael stood up and walked toward the tray that our food was delivered on and carefully pulled up the table cloth. A bomb! I could not believe this, just when I thought all the drama was over. When I stood up, I was frozen. I didn't know what to do with myself. I waited for Rafael to say something to me. He didn't move and then all of a sudden he grabbed his cell phone and pushed one button. He took a picture of the bomb and started talking to the other person on the line.

"Maya, go outside and find the nearest fire alarm. Listen for me to tell you when to pull it. Just in case. There is still twenty minutes on the timer. Don't worry. I can do this with my eyes closed." Rafael nodded his head for me to go. His voice was so harsh; I could hear him down the hall. I felt bad for whoever he was talking to. Several minutes later I heard him call out the condo door, "All clear."

I had so many thoughts going through my head in those few minutes, I felt out of my mind. I walked back inside the door. He had the bomb disabled and started giving instructions to an agent to dispose the ordnance.

I walked straight out to the balcony for a cigarette and after I lit one, sat down. I looked up to the clear sky, then to the horizon where the sea met the sky. It was so beautiful here and I wondered if I would ever come back. It would never be the same to me. This whole experience has changed my life forever. I was caught up in my own thoughts when Rafael came up behind me and kissed the top of my head. He went back inside and grabbed our two cups of coffee and came out on the balcony. He sat down, took a sip and put his cup down. He looked at me with these determined eyes, and I just sat waiting for him to tell me what was going on. He reached for one of my cigarettes and lit it, sat back in his chair, and finally said,

"We are going to Spain tonight."

"What?"

"My team is on their way now. You and I are taking a private jet to a small airport near Huelva, and my team will meet us there and take us to a private villa. We already have people in Spain to help with the details, and more manpower."

"I can't just go to Spain; I don't even have a passport."

"You will by the time we leave tonight."

"Why do I have to go?"

"I can't protect you if you're not with me, and since you are involved in this case, I need you."

"Need me for what?" I was confused.

"There is a ball tomorrow night. The man behind this whole case will be there, and we need to get him while he is away from his fortress. It may be our only chance to get to him. You, as my wife, and I are now on the guest list. I just need you to trust me and listen to what I say."

"You know you promised me that I was going to get to do all the things I came here to do. I thought this was all over. Now I'm going to Spain and playing your wife in some CIA operation." He smiled at my attempt to give him some of my attitude. Then I smiled at the sweet, pleading, almost begging look on his face.

"Okay but I have to be home by Sunday. It's Halloween and I don't want to miss that."

"I promise to have you home on Sunday." He stood up and leaned into my face and kissed me, strong and hard. I wondered what that was all about, but only for about ten seconds. Then his lips kissed the skin under my chin and neck.

"Thank you for doing this. I can't even think about leaving you now and not making love to you again."

He was just staring into my eyes, and I melted every time he looked at me like that.

"Well making love to me now won't be the last time." I returned his look and smiled, and in a split second he was picking me up and carrying me to the couch and laying me down. He undid my robe that was barely tied to begin with and opened each side looking at every part of me. He had this amazing way of making me feel so sexy. I was putty in his hands. He placed himself on top of me and went for my neck. I felt him against me, and I increased my own intensity. I found his lips and opened mine to invite his tongue to dance. I felt the strength in his shoulders and back and moved my hands down to his shorts. I pulled them down and reached for him. He was so hard, and I felt him pulsing in my hand as I stroked the length of him. His lips were still playing with mine and we made eye contact. His face looked pained.

"What's wrong?"

"I don't want there to ever be a last time."

He pulled his shorts all the way off and parted my legs. Teasing me with his penis, rubbing himself against me and tracing my opening with the tip of his erection, I thought I was going to die if I didn't have him right then. I lifted my leg and grabbed his butt pulling him down on me and inside me. The electric shock could have cured any neurological problem I may have had. He pushed himself all the way inside me and held it. We kissed some gentle kisses, and I realized the pure passion that existed in this moment. I will never forget that feeling. I have only ever felt this way with my husband before now, and I was remembering the way it was when Matt and I first started dating, this wanting for someone else physically and feeling aroused all the time, the way most couples start out but struggle to maintain. Rafael definitely aroused every sense in my body and mind and soul. I knew it was going to be short lived, and I also knew this was going to change my life. However wrong and devious this whole thing was, I wanted to learn from it and experience all of it.

He started moving slowly inside me and my thoughts returned to Rafael and how he was making me feel right now. We were still keeping eye contact until I closed my eyes and felt him, all of him, his skin touching so much of me in so many places. I was overwhelmed and feeling myself raising my hips to meet him when he pulled out the slightest bit. I wasn't holding anything back, and I was moaning a sweet cry wanting more, to fall off the edge and finish the intensity that was building in my body. I opened my eyes and my mouth at the same time and saw him watching my face and feeling the beginning of my climax. He sped up to release his own passion with me. My hands were tied up in his hair and pulling his mouth to mine. I was devouring him, all of him, and letting go of anything that seemed taboo. I felt him so hot inside me, and sharing the after climax sensations together was amazing. He pulled away so he could look at me, that incredible look of hunger in his eyes.

With his arm around my waist, he pulled me up with him and sat up on the couch keeping me on top of him so that I was sitting on his lap facing him. I felt him still hard inside of me and the wetness between us. He was so beautiful to look at. I put my hands back in his hair, pushing it away from his face and kissing him as gently and sweetly as he had kissed me. I rocked a little on top of him and still felt him stretching me, filling me. He was ready to go again and so was I, but I really needed to know what was going on and the whole going to Spain plan. I kept moving on top of him and kept my grip in his hair, then I whispered in his ear.

"Tell me about Spain."

12
Chapter

"It's beautiful there, you will love it."

I kissed him again then pulled away to let him finish.

"There are gorgeous beaches and hotels and bougainvilleas growing against every wall. The sunsets are even more sensual then here, but you'll have to see for yourself. All the plans have been taken care of. The only thing we have to do is attend a gala in black tie and check out the security in the building. Easy. There will be two teams there to take down the buyer that wanted the flash drive. It turns out that he has been watched by the CIA and FBI for using the port near Huelva to smuggle guns and drugs."

"Have you been there before?"

"Only one time. I was just passing through," Rafael said, but I had the feeling there was more to that comment.

"Then I guess we will share the beauty together."

My mind wasn't on the operation or the CIA or FBI or the landscaping in Huelva, it was on my breasts now rubbing against his chest. My nipples were hard and touching his as I moved a little faster on him using my knees for leverage on the couch. I leaned back taking all of him inside me and moaned so softly. I felt his fingers rubbing my sex and the wetness let his fingers glide along the center of me. I could feel my own erection at the touch of his fingers. I wanted to come, I was so close and he slowed the movement of his fingers and started kissing and sucking my nipples, sending more sensual shock to my body. He grabbed my legs and wrapped them around his waist and stood up. He took me to the bedroom, sat me down on the edge of the bed, and pulled himself out of me. I lay back and he knelt down and tasted me, tasted both of our passion and teased me with his tongue. I was on the edge again. He could feel me wanting more and slowed down instantly. I thought I was going to scream. His tongue found a trail up to my breasts and that was the only part of him that was touching me as he hovered over me. I closed my eyes and couldn't believe how alive I felt. I felt beautiful and sexy and wanted. He was at my neck and found my lips as he lowered himself on top of me. I felt his erection pressing against me and then easing inside of me as slowly as he kissed me. This felt different, emotionally deeper and difficult to describe. He made love to me and finally from the sheer erotic need for my release, I came softly and it lasted for hours. I never left the point of climax. He made love to me over and over and I never stopped my first climax. It just continued through the duration until we couldn't move another muscle. We fell asleep in that position until his phone rang. As if it weren't important, he kissed me so intensely, then lifted himself off the bed and reached for his phone.

"Yes." Rafael listened while he was still looking at me, and then said, "We'll be ready."

Then he hung up. He gave me that serious but sneaky smile and said to me, "We have two hours before the jet leaves."

"We should probably take a shower." I smiled at him the same way he was smiling at me, and I got up to go to the bathroom and turned on the water for the shower. Rafael crawled back in bed for a few minutes giving me some time to myself in the bathroom. When he heard the shower door open, he walked into the bathroom and I stepped into the shower. He joined me. The hot water made my body feel weak, and we managed to steam the entire bathroom in minutes. We showered and washed each other, and as I was tilting my head back to rinse the conditioner from my hair, I felt him behind me. His hands moved from my waist to my breasts, and I rested the back of my head against his shoulder. I was so relaxed and exhausted I could hardly move. He moved one hand to my navel and then lower touching me between my legs. I reached my arm around his to the side of his body and pulled him closer to my back side. He started kissing my neck as he reached for himself behind me. I was barely on my toes when he slid his erection inside me; the force of it lifted me up. He continued playing with my nipples and touching me where our bodies connected. I reached for his hand and intertwined my fingers with his. I was touching myself with him, feeling him entering me and pulling out, massaging my flesh with our fingers, and I could feel him giving into his need to come, like he couldn't stop it. He cried my name, and I reached behind his neck to turn his head, and our kisses found each other's neck and mouth as I felt him let go. He slowly stopped and rested his forehead on my shoulder. The water was getting cooler but still drenching us in the warmth and steam that consumed the bathroom. He reached for the knob and turned the faucet off. Then he pulled himself out of me and turned me to face him. He touched his hands to both sides of my face and pulled me to his mouth. One long very sensual kiss and I was literally weak. He picked me up and carried me to the bed soaking wet, lay me down and covered me with the comforter. I remember thinking how the bed smelt like jasmine, and I drifted off to sleep.

Chapter 13

"Maya." Rafael whispered in my ear. I was always a very light sleeper; I opened my eyes and smiled at him.

"Hi." I said and realized he was fully dressed. "Is it time to go?"

"Yes, I have all your things packed. All you need to do is pick something to wear on the plane. Kit had a blast today shopping in Spain for clothes for you and for anything you could possibly need while we're there. I have someone driving your Jeep and your things to Tampa International Airport, so you won't have far to drive home."

New clothes, wow. I couldn't remember the last time I bought myself a new outfit. Actually I couldn't remember the last time I bought myself anything, other than a new bathing suit for this vacation, not because I didn't like to shop, simply because to get by on one income I pinched every penny. I knew Matt would have to work harder if I spent too much.

I just hoped they all fit!

"What about a gown for tomorrow night?"

"Already taken care of." He held out his hand to help me up and I took it.

"Move over Cinderella, Maya is on her way!"

I walked into the bathroom and Rafael went to the kitchen. I looked at myself in the mirror and the look in my eyes was different. Maybe the adrenalin highs these last few days had finally caught up with my body, and I looked beautiful and tired. I brushed my teeth and washed my face.

Rafael walked in with a glass of wine and handed it to me.

I was totally naked standing in the bathroom sipping a glass of wine in the company of this gorgeous man, just staring at me, and I felt like a queen, like this was a normal daily activity. I laughed to myself and looked at Rafael.

"What's so funny?" he asked with a weird look on his face.

"I was just thinking how crazy all of this is. I mean, my life at home is so structured and planned, and this is like an erotic action movie."

"I'm impressed with everything about you, but mostly at how you've kept your composure through all of this. I admire your strength, your quick wit, and I still haven't forgotten how you took out those two hired guns at the warehouse. You amaze me with everything that you are and do, and everything you have shared with me."

"I can't even tell you the things I have learned about myself here with you. Thank you."

He kissed me and left me in the bathroom. I grabbed a pair of capri pants, a light sweater, socks and my slip in sneakers, and was dressed in no time. One last thing, my baseball hat, and not because I'm into baseball, but because then I didn't have to worry about my hair.

I went out to the balcony and sat with my wine and smoked a cigarette before we had to go. Rafael came out and sat with me. He was just looking out to the ocean and was quiet.

"Is something wrong?" I asked.

"I can't bring myself to regret these last few days with you, but I'm sorry I got you into this. I shouldn't want you to come to Spain. If something should happen to you, I would never forgive myself. I don't want to leave you yet. I am being very selfish."

"I don't see it like that at all. I've enjoyed every minute I have been here with you. I may never get the chance to go to Spain. This has all been quite an adventure, I'll say that!"

"How is it that you can still be so beautiful and sexy in a baseball hat?" He just smiled at me with those beautiful eyes.

"It's a talent!" We both laughed.

"We have about an eight-hour flight, which leaves in an hour, so you have some time to enjoy your wine and have some peace. I have some calls to make and details to work out with the agents in Spain, so I'll leave you to yourself."

He stood up and leaned down to kiss me, then he ran his finger along the split in my lip that was healing pretty well. I hid it with a tinted lip gloss and you could barely even see where it was. He walked to the counter in the kitchen and sat down on a bar stool. He picked up his phone and was talking immediately to someone in Spanish.

I wasn't paying attention to the conversation because thoughts like "What the hell am I doing?" kept running through my head. I lit the last of the synthetic marijuana I rolled and smoked what was left of it, sipping my wine and trying to clear my mind. I was terrified inside while trying to be strong on the outside. I was going to be fine. I am strong and stubborn I thought, and was born with an attitude.

I would be home on Sunday to give out candy on Halloween while Matt and Hayden went trick or treating. In our neighborhood it was more fun for the adults than the kids, even though Halloween wasn't my favorite holiday. I didn't have to worry about a costume because Hayden wanted to be Spiderman again, so we had the costume from last year. He actually wore it around the house all the time. I was usually the bad superhero, fighting with light sabers until the death. My day wouldn't be the same without those moments. I hoped that Matt and Hayden were having a good time together. I could only imagine the condition of the house right now.

I finished my glass of wine and noticed that all was quiet in the condo. I turned around in my chair and saw Rafael just standing behind me, watching me, smiling. I smiled back and just looked at him. He was so amazingly beautiful. I still couldn't believe all of this was happening to me.

Chapter 14

"Are you ready to go?" he said still smiling at me.

"What if I say no?" I tried to look serious.

We left everything except for what we were wearing. It was such a weird feeling, knowing that in a few more days, all of my things and my Jeep would be in Tampa waiting for me. Now I was going to Spain to help in an operation for the CIA to take down a drug and weapons smuggler. This just wasn't real. Things like this just didn't happen to the average stay-at-home-mom, but then again I wasn't just a stay-at-home-mom anymore. I was a woman with passion and self-worth again. I was leaving this place a different person than when I came.

We walked out the door and to the elevators. When we were inside he kissed me so intensely as if it were to be our last kiss here. Remembering the last few days, and kissing like we were saying goodbye to the place that brought us together.

We got out and went through the lobby to the front doors where there was a car waiting for us. Two agents were in the front seats, so Rafael opened the back door for me to get in and walked over to the other side and got in. I looked up to the building and said goodbye in my mind. We pulled away from the condos and drove down the main road. I just looked out the window and rode quietly until we reached the small airport. We drove right up to the jet, and the four of us walked up the stairs to the door. I went in first and my eyes were wide when I saw the inside. It had everything, a small kitchen area with curtains that opened up to the main room that had couches and tables with recliners facing them. I sat on the couch and took my cap off. Rafael and the two other agents sat at the table and chairs, opened their laptops, and started talking.

The sun was starting to set and the sky was so beautiful and warm with color. I felt like I could sleep some more. I slid down and rested my head on the arm of the sofa. Rafael stood and walked to a closet and brought me a blanket.

"Thank you."

"Let me know if you want anything. I just have some things to tend to, and then I'm all yours."

"Now, how am I supposed to rest knowing that?" I teased him.

"That reminds me, Kit didn't know what kind of underwear you wore." He looked almost embarrassed.

"Tell her not to worry about it because I never wear them while on special missions."

"Now how am I supposed to get any work done knowing that?"

"You asked." I laughed and noticed that Rafael looked happy. He looked different from the first time I saw him at the bar outside the condo. I imagined I looked different too. He kissed me and went back to the table with a look of desperation in his smile.

I was really tired and didn't even notice when we took off and were in the air. I hated flying. I wondered if he had any idea of how brave I felt inside right now. I woke up at the sound of Rafael whispering in my ear.

"Are you hungry?"

"No," I answered with my eyes still closed.

"Would you like some wine?"

"Love some."

He returned with two glasses and a bottle of wine. I sat up and crossed my legs, facing him sitting next to me on the sofa. I took a sip when he handed me my glass and put it down in my lap, playing with the top of the glass with my fingertips.

"How are you holding up?" he asked as he touched the side of my cheek with his hand.

"I'm fine." I raised my hand to touch his face in return.

His skin was as soft as silk and always smelled so manly.

"Tell me more about you."

"Ask me what you want to know," I said.

"Why a Jeep?"

"I love the freedom of feeling the wind in my hair. It's a four door, and it's my favorite shade of putrid green. I like the fact that it's not a car, or a truck. It's different."

"How do you know self-defense moves?"

"Every woman should know how to defend herself and her family."

"Why did you come to Panama City Beach?"

"I just needed a break from my life, to reflect and relax." I looked down at my glass and then back to his gaze. "What I have gotten out of this so far is that I have sacrificed so much of myself to my family that I have forgotten that I am a strong and beautiful woman. I used to be that person. I used my sexuality to get things. I always felt like a woman until I got married and had Hayden, then pieces of that woman were replaced by having to be a wife and mother. I had forgotten what it felt like to be a woman first. You have given me that part of myself back, and you make me feel beautiful and sexy, the way I used to feel about myself."

It was all true. I came wondering what had happened to my marriage, wanting to see the bigger picture, and how much I loved my family. I did that in finding myself again. I would go home a better person. How this would affect my marriage I still wasn't sure.

"I'm sorry about your mother, too." Rafael said.

"It's funny how after 10 years, I still want to call her when good things happen or I just need to talk." Now I have Anne-Marie and my dad, Matt's parents, and our neighbors, Nana and Gero, who are like adopted grandparents to Hayden. Nana was like a mother figure to me. Matt and I called her 'the calming voice of reason'. We always felt lucky to have so much support and love between our families. I looked away from him for a minute and then said, "You and your mother must have been very close."

I didn't want to ask about his father because he had never brought him up before. I had sensed some deep sensitivity so I avoided the subject. Maybe it wasn't the best story to share. I respected the things he did share, and I took notice of the way he spoke, as if he'd never told anyone these stories before. It seemed he had no one close enough to have conversations like these.

"Yes, we were all we had, each other. It was very hard for me when she died, but now this life is the only thing I know."

"Rafael, you are such a beautiful person, and you could find love and have a normal life."

"Maya, I told you I had never thought about a family or love until I met you. Now having experienced the things we have shared together, I'm not sure anyone could ever make me feel the way you do. I could spend the rest of my life looking for someone, and I would never find the one that would be as amazing as you are. You are so special to me, even if I never find someone else; I will always have these memories to hold on to. That would be good enough for me." He finished and leaned over to kiss me.

I felt sad for him. He could make a woman very happy, I could attest to that. Then, I remembered that things are always exciting in the beginning and then everything changes. Love changes. At the same time, love and admiration grow deeper and more important. That's what makes a family and marriage stronger than ever. I wanted that for Rafael as much as I wanted that for myself.

We kissed for a long time, just touching our lips, feeling each other's breath. I closed my eyes, feeling his mouth and tongue and the warmth that permeated my body. It was nice just kissing, knowing right now it couldn't go farther. It was just adding to the anticipation of later, when we could be alone in Spain.

Rafael walked over to the closet and grabbed a pillow. The two other agents were reclined in their chairs with the lights out and headphones on. Rafael walked back to me, took the glass from my hand, and set it down on the side table. He pulled the couch and the back folded down. I imagined people needed to sleep on long flights; of course there would be a bed. He laid the pillow down and said,

"We should really get some sleep."

I lay down and he snuggled up next to me. I was lying on my back and he was on his side. His face was an inch away from mine. He pulled up the blanket and rolled one of his legs over the top of mine. I felt his lips getting closer to mine.

"I thought we needed to sleep?"

"This will help you!"

His hand went under the elastic waist band of my capri pants, and he realized I wasn't playing around when I said I wasn't wearing underwear. He grinned and nudged my face to the side to play with my ear. That and the neck were my weak points; he obviously knew that by now. The sensation gave me the goose bumps which in turn made my nipples hard. I saw the moon outside the window lighting up the night. It was extraordinary and seemed close enough that I could reach out and touch it. He moved his fingers in all the right places, making me wet and wanting to moan. Trying to stay quiet was going to be a challenge since we were not alone. Ask me if I cared right then! He slipped his fingers inside me and used his thumb to stimulate me. I needed more.

"Make love to me."

"I just want to give you pleasure and watch you enjoy it."

Well I was enjoying it and it didn't take long with the exquisite touch of his fingers to make me explode with satisfaction. He continued touching me and kissing me, and I felt like I could sleep now, having released any tension I might have had. He laid his head next to mine, wrapped his arm around me, and closed his own eyes. I could still hear the arousal in our breathing as it started to slow down. I could still feel the pulse in his leg beating as hard as mine. I lay there recovering and tried not to think of anything else. It wasn't easy. I looked back to see the moon and I soon drifted off to sleep.

I started dreaming of Matt and Hayden. I always had this recurring dream of being in a crowd and not being able to find them. I understood why, it was obvious the meaning was that I was afraid to lose them.

Chapter 15

"Maya, are you awake?"

"Kinda."

"Look outside," he whispered in my ear.

It was the most colorful and stunning sunrise I had ever seen. He pulled me closer to his body and we watched the sun rise slowly. He kissed the side of my face and propped his head up to look out the window and watch the sun. His cheek felt rough against mine. Morning stubble. Still he softly rubbed his face along my face and jaw line. I just stared out the window at the beauty of the water and brilliant colors of the sun and the sky.

We heard the two other agents moving around and one got up to use the bathroom. I could smell coffee brewing and took a deep breath of the aroma. Rafael and I lay there looking out the window.

"Would you like some coffee?"

"Yes, thank you." Now it was clear I was being spoiled. I know he felt guilty for this whole mess, but I was starting to get used to being pampered and waited on all the time. I should enjoy this too, while it lasted. Matt had never in all the years we'd been together, made me a cup of coffee and brought it to me.

I got up and went to the bathroom. As I looked in the mirror, I was surprised to see a glow even after everything I had been through. I freshened up my face and messed with my hair a little before I went back out. There were fresh breads and pastries with the coffee on the large rectangular table where Rafael and the other agents were sitting. Rafael stood and swiveled a chair for me to sit in at the table and then sat down himself.

"Maya, this is special agent Martin, and special agent Duvall. I apologize for not introducing them earlier."

"Good morning." I said and they just nodded.

Rafael and the two agents talked a little about some of the details of their plans, while I sipped my coffee and picked at a croissant. Again they were speaking Spanish, but I was really paying attention to what they were saying. I picked up that the CIA's target name was Luis Sanchez, and they had a platoon of armed bodyguards guarding him at all times. This event was one of the few opportunities when he would be out in the open and away from his fortified home. They said he was a very dangerous man and associated with the seediest thugs in Spain while running guns and drugs out of the port he owned in Huelva. He apparently owned most of the town and surrounding areas. He sounded pretty powerful to me. Again, why was I doing this, I thought.

I should have just stayed in Florida on the beach and been done with all of this. Clearly my mind was not working correctly. Not that it ever did. I actually had a way of rationalizing with myself into thinking that Almond Joy candy bars were healthy because they had milk chocolate for the dairy group, coconut for the fruit group, and almonds for the protein group. Three food groups in one small snack. It was like a meal to me. That must be what I was doing now, here on this jet to Spain. I was rationalizing this so that I could feel powerful as a woman again. I absolutely needed this. I wanted to enjoy it because I knew the guilt and remorse would come later.

I must have been making faces while I was talking to myself in my head because when I looked up at Rafael and the others, they were all grinning at me.

"What?" I asked literally embarrassed.

"What were you thinking about?" Rafael asked.

"Dancing the tango," I said. "Do you know how to tango?"

"Yes, and we will." He smiled with a devilish twinkle in his eyes, and the other agents chuckled. One of them made a comment to Rafael and they all laughed. I acted like I didn't care what he said, which in English, was that we already acted like a newlywed couple. With our new identities, we were honeymooning in Spain and were invited to this grand gala by one of the politicians attending. This was going to be easy if this was how I was supposed to act for the next several days.

"Do I have a different name with my passport and papers?"

"Would you like to see them?"

"Yes." I was excited to be someone else for a few days.

Rafael reached into the duffel bag next to the chair, pulled out two manila envelopes, and handed them to me. The first one I opened was his. His name was Rafael Montoya. I wondered what his real name was; surely he didn't use his own name in the CIA. Then I opened the other. My new name was Angel Montoya. Reading further in the file, I learned we were recently married; lived in California where Rafael worked for the court system, and I volunteered most of my time with children and seniors in the hospitals.

Wow, I was more than an angel; I was a Saint in this report. I wondered what kind of mastermind came up with this scenario. Rafael cleared his throat, and I looked up at him.

"Everything looks good to me!" I enthusiastically approved. I obviously had no idea what I was doing, or going to be doing. It was exciting and I loved it. All of it. True to the roller coaster ride that was the past few days, I felt like I had more of a purpose than cleaning and laundry.

"Great. We will be landing in about an hour," Rafael said.

"Would you mind if I used your laptop to check my email, just to make sure there is nothing important I need to respond to?"

"Sure." Rafael slid the laptop in front of him toward me and I opened it.

The three of them kept talking, but I wasn't paying attention at all. I went to my email account and had one hundred and sixty seven emails. Most of them I deleted, but every day I got a tarot card reading sent to me. When I finished deleting almost everything, I clicked on my reading for today. The Eight of Chalices card suggested "my power today lies in space. I am true to myself and will only regret the chances I don't take to seek or follow my heart's desire. I turn away from or make a clean sweep of that which does not honor or sustain my passion and love, and in this, I am not afraid to be alone. I am empowered to move forward or make space and my gift is letting go." Well that tells me everything I need to know. I closed out my email and shut the laptop.

"Thank you."

"Anything important?"

"No."

"I think the moon shared its glow with you last night. You look absolutely radiant."

"I think it's all the exercise I've had lately." I couldn't keep from smiling at him.

"I know this may sound weird but the guys always get a pool going on these types of operations. Like how many people get shot, or how many shots are fired. Just a little friendly competition to make things more interesting. I need to know what your lucky number is."

That made me feel very reassured that this was going to be a safe mission. I gave them all a dirty look, as if I didn't approve.

"It is two."

"What makes two lucky for you?" he wondered.

Agents Martin and Duvall seemed as interested in my reason as Rafael was.

"Well on March 2, 1971 I was born and became a daughter. On March 2, 2003 I met my husband and became a wife, and on March 2, 2006 my son was born and I became a mother." I was looking at them and the looks on their faces were priceless. Men could be so sensitive sometimes. I smiled at the genuine feelings that came from these big, tough CIA agents.

"You are quite a woman, Mrs. Montoya," Rafael said and then asked the other agents if they wouldn't mind if we had a few minutes to ourselves. They happily left the room through another draped partition. He thanked them and got up from his chair, knelt on the floor, and rested his head in my lap. I touched his hair and moved it away from the side of his face. He looked up at me and said,

"Are you sure you're okay with all of this?"

"I'm doing very well, thank you." Actually I was terrified that when all of this finally caught up to me, I might just break down.

"Are you scared?"

"No. I know everything will be fine, as long as I have you protecting me, and making love to me, and in the end the bad guy gets caught, right?"

"You haven't stopped surprising me since the moment I met you! I can't wait to see what you pull off at the ball tomorrow." I contained my laughter but managed a smile, completely terrified on the inside. I could always hide my feelings on the outside. I was the perfect poker player. Rafael reached up and touched the dimples on my face.

My mother told me when I was younger that my dimples were kisses from the angels. I would like to know what they were doing on the back of my thighs and butt.

"Nor have you stopped surprising me, Mr. Montoya." I laid my head against the back of the recliner, and Rafael just stayed curled up in my lap holding the sides of my legs.

The pilot's voice came over the intercom and informed us we would be landing in about thirty minutes, and our transportation was ready and waiting upon our arrival. Rafael sat back in his own chair and held my hand. We just sat quietly and enjoyed the peace and our own thoughts until we arrived at the airport. No wonder I didn't feel us leave the ground. The landing was as motionless as the takeoff. We came to a stop, the door with the stairs opened, and the two other agents went down the steps. Rafael and I were still sitting, holding hands, and smiling at each other.

16
Chapter

"Shall we, my beautiful wife?"

"You know arranged marriages don't exist in this country." I smiled and we stood up and walked to the door and down the stairs. It felt unfamiliar not having a single bag, just us and what we were wearing.

His team got out of the SUV and walked to meet us. There were three of them including Kit. Techno must be busy getting ready and setting up all his communications and computers. Kit hugged me, and Rock and Tex kissed me on each side of my face. With Rafael they were all business. We started walking toward the vehicle, and they were already deep into the details of the mission, important information, and times for each part of the operation. I understood most of it. Nothing I didn't already know except for the timeline of events. Funny, I knew this, but had no idea what time or day it was right now. We all got in the SUV and Rafael, Kit and I sat in the back. Kit was so thrilled to tell me how much fun it was to shop for someone else, telling me she never had family or siblings to buy things for. So she was happy to finally have someone to shop for. She made me laugh so hard I thought I was going to pee myself. This happens after childbirth, something that no one tells you about ahead of time. My hand found Rafael's and it felt as natural as grabbing for my husband's hand. He snickered under his breath about Kit and me, but I didn't care because the rush of the unknown was sweeping through my body. From what I understood from one of the previous conversations, Rafael and I were staying in a private villa, and the rest of the crew had rooms at the resort just down the road. The ride from the airport to the villa was about a twenty-minute scenic drive through the countryside.

We arrived at the private villa first. I could only see a few tall buildings a mile down the road, and everyone got out and came inside. It was breathtaking. The fountains and gardens surrounding the front of the villa looked like they were straight out of a House and Garden magazine. We walked up a few natural stone steps to the impressive ten foot tall front door with a high arch at the top. I walked inside and it was twice the size of my house. The floors were all polished marble. The furniture was exquisite, intricately carved wood tables and chairs. There were indoor palms and plants and flowers on every table and in huge pots sitting on the floor.

I went to the kitchen and opened the refrigerator. It was stocked with fresh fruits, alcohol, and some already made dishes covered with saran wrap. I asked everyone if I could make them something to eat or drink, and Rafael turned around.

"This is our honeymoon darling; you're the one who is getting all the pampering for the next five days. Sit down and we'll call in some food." He pulled out some menus and called in the order. "We have some things to get set up and a few small details to talk about. There is a bottle of chilled Chardonnay, if you would like a glass."

He was already opening the bottle and smiling at me when I answered,

"You've come to know me so well."

He gave me the glass and kissed me so hard I would have been embarrassed if anyone was watching. Maybe not.

I walked through the back of the villa and went out to the deck as wide as the villa. There were lounge chairs, outdoor couches and seating areas with a table and chairs all along the deck which overlooked a ridge of land and the coast beyond that. I picked a lounge chair and set my wine on the table next to it. I was mesmerized by the colors and smells of the ocean and waves. The view from this level was spectacular, just as Rafael had described the gorgeous landscaping, cliffs, and the ocean below. It looked like a postcard photo. I sipped my wine and was reminded of one of my dearest friends, whom I was always thought of whenever I drank chardonnay. Kay had been like a mentor to me for at least fifteen years now. I met her when she was a nail client of mine and we grew very close. Whenever I would go to her house, she always had a bottle of chardonnay chilled and waiting. We would sit for hours talking, laughing, and singing. She knew me better that anyone from the inside out. We shared a lot of good times together and probably as many bad. I wondered what she was up to these days. I moved away from that area years ago and we only got together a couple of times a year now. I really missed her. She had always been one of the most inspiring people I had ever known. It would be interesting to ponder what Kay would have thought about all of this. I smiled and was back to the scenery.

I noticed on one of the tables there was an ashtray and a pack of my cigarettes. God bless Kit! I walked over to retrieve them, and when I turned around I said out loud,

"Speak of the devil!"

Kit was laying in the lounge chair next to mine and was smiling. She was so cute and lively.

"Kit, I really want to thank you for everything you have done. I adore you, and I'm really thankful that we've met."

"Are you kidding. This is one of the most fun jobs we've ever had! You can thank the whole team. It seems they adore you as well. They all helped in getting things for you. We've really enjoyed getting to know you, and we should be thanking you. It's not often that our jobs become personal."

"What about Rafael?"

"What about him?" She was smiling and started to laugh.

"Tell me about him."

"Well Maya, before you walked into all of our lives, my dear friend Rafael had been all work. He lived for this job and I'd never seen him let loose until now. I mean he's still all business with all of this going on, but you have shown him your heart. You've shown all of us your heart and bravery in how you have handled this situation. In this profession we don't get the opportunity to get close to people. In our line of work it's hard to have spouses or families. We are each other's family here. Rafael has found his heart because of you and you reminded the rest of us that we do need love. I am so happy for Rafael; we are all sharing in his happiness."

"Until recently I couldn't figure out what I was missing in my life when it seemed so full yet so lonely. Rafael has made me feel like a woman again and that's something I will never forget."

"Maya you are quite a woman. You have impressed the CIA, won the hearts of everyone on this team, and if I may say so, you have been an inspiration to me. Your family is very lucky."

"I know, but I am really the lucky one."

"Well, the guys are going to finish up soon and we'll be out of your hair."

"Kit, would you like to join me with a glass of wine and a cigarette?"

"I thought you'd never ask!"

I hopped up, headed to the kitchen, found a wine glass after searching every cabinet in the massive kitchen, poured Kit some wine, and returned to the deck. I handed her the glass and pulled my lounge chair closer to Kit. I reached for my glass and we toasted to the beauty and passion of Spain. We both drank to that, and I opened the pack of cigarettes. Two cigarettes were missing and two hand rolled ones in their place. I looked up to her with a questioning face.

"I took the liberty to get the real marijuana." We both started laughing so hard, and I pulled one of the hand rolled ones out of the pack and lit it. I motioned to it and raised my eyebrows to invite her to share with me, and she took it willingly. We talked and laughed and it seemed like hours had passed when the rest of the team came outside. Rafael had the rest of the bottle and some additional glasses, and we all sat on the deck smoking and drinking and laughing hysterically about nothing really. The effects of the pot made us all giggly. They were all very close to each other; you could tell by the way they interacted. I felt like I was a part of their team, like I belonged. I learned the story about how Kit got her name. She was so tiny and vicious when she started that they called her Kitty and then Kit for short. They all shared the greatest stories, and I even shared some funny moments of my own, mostly about my son and the crazy things that come out of his mouth sometimes. Maybe it was the scenery or the company, but it seemed like we didn't have a care in the world right now, and it was delightful. I looked at Rafael with beaming eyes, and I saw him make deliberate eye contact with Rock. I quickly glanced at Rock, and he nodded his head. Seconds later they were standing up and saying they had to get going. Each of them came to me and kissed my cheeks, and I thanked them all for everything. I swear it seemed like it happened in warp speed, and when they were all up and heading to the door, I blurted,

"Voy a ver a todos ustedes por breakfast y café en la manana, no demasaido pronto."

It just came out, like the old adage when in Rome, act like a Roman. I don't know, it just came out. The English translation was that I invited them all for breakfast and coffee in the morning, but not too early.

Rafael and the other members of the team stopped dead in their tracks and turned around and started walking back toward where I was standing, and they stared at me. It was a little awkward at first until I realized I just spoke to them in Spanish. It seemed like as good a time as any to let them in on my little secret.

"Despues de nueve?" I said, "After nine." I couldn't help but smile, and it was difficult trying to keep from bursting with laughter. I was hoping that someone else would say something soon.

They started laughing, and I was just so relieved the attention wasn't directed at me anymore, so I let go and laughed along with them

"You speak Spanish?" Rafael asked with amazement.

"Si Senor Montoya." Everyone was still laughing except Rafael. I kept my eyes on him and walked up to him. I kissed him and whispered in his ear, "I love when you tell me what you are going to do to me in Spanish."

17

Chapter

He started kissing me, and I barely heard the team excusing themselves and closing the door behind them. I could feel the beating of his heart against my chest, and for as long as I could concentrate, our hearts were beating to the same rhythm with the same quickness, the same excitement, and then I lost myself in Rafael's kisses. His mouth was so hot and soft, and I wanted to kiss him for hours. I knew I couldn't wait that long, and I had a distinct feeling he couldn't either.

The doorbell rang and Rafael broke away from me, pushed me to the side, and pulled his gun. He opened the door and it was our food. I peeked around the corner to see Rafael paying the delivery man, and I started giggling. He brought the bags into the kitchen and we both laughed.

"Do you think that everyone who comes to the door is going to kill you?" I couldn't stop laughing.

"Yes."

We laughed again and started opening all the bags of food. We had completely forgotten about ordering food an hour ago. Now we had all this authentic Spanish food, and it was just the two of us.

Rafael looked at me seriously for a moment and I smiled.

"Were you going to tell me that you spoke Spanish?"

"Yes, but probably not until I had to leave. Like I said, I love when you whisper in my ear, especially in Spanish. With your tender accent and devilish words, you turn me into mush every time. I hope you won't stop now that you know I understand what you're saying."

"Now that I know all of that, I will definitely do it more!"

"I look forward to it," I said smiling.

Rafael opened a bottle of Merlot and we sampled all the wonderful food. At least now we didn't have to worry about dinner. We walked out to the deck, sat on the loveseat and propped our feet on the table, then gazed at the sea. It was a moment to remember. Sharing this with Rafael was magnificent. Spain was never a place I had ever dreamed of visiting, but I wouldn't have given up this experience for anything. I mean you only live once, right? Having an erotic affair with a man in Spain is not something I ever thought would happen in my simple life.

"Want to go for a walk on the beach?" Rafael asked me.

"Can we get down there from here?" I asked rather surprised.

We slipped off our shoes and socks, then he rolled up his pants, took me by the hand, and we went to the end of the deck to a flight of stairs leading down to the gardens. The grass was so soft and the layers of flowers and palm trees made this area very private. We stood there for a minute taking in the shocking beauty and then walked closer to the edge of the rock cliff to another flight of stairs down the ridge of rock to the beach. There wasn't another soul on the private beach for as far as I could see in either direction. The breeze was soft and the air was warm and dry, unlike the Central Florida humidity. We walked along the shoreline, and the water was refreshing and cool, but not cold.

"So what does it feel like being Mrs. Angel Montoya?" Rafael broke the silence.

"Well, I haven't had my honeymoon yet, so I'll have to get back to you on that." I smirked, giving him the green light to touch me. He grabbed me around the waist and pulled me hard into his chest, and his mouth took mine like it belonged to him. He stopped kissing me and the back of his fingertips caressed the side of my face.

"I'm in love with you, Mrs. Montoya." He watched for a reaction and stared into my eyes. He knew my heart belonged to someone else, and what we had now was all we would ever have, but he looked at me hoping for a chance for something different.

"I love you too, and I promise you that as long as we are together, I will love you in every way I can, and no matter what, you will always be in my heart. I will never forget you."

"I'll take that." I could see the faint disappointment in his eyes.

I leaned up to him and kissed him, feeling the constant rush of wind touching and bending around the sides of our faces. I looked him in the eyes as I kissed him harder, letting him know I wanted more. I started unbuttoning his shirt and pulled it off, feeling his chest and his abdominals as I reached for his pants button. He kept my eye contact the whole time. I loved that, kissing and just looking at each other in the eye, seeing into the other. I unzipped his pants and they dropped to the sand. I moved my kisses to his nipples and down the center of his stomach, pulling his boxer briefs past his knees until they fell on their own. I stood tall and found his mouth with mine again. He pulled my sweater over my head and dropped it to the sand. He reached around to my bra and undid the hook. His hands moved to my shoulders where he slid the straps down my arms until they fell. He lowered himself down on his knees and kissed my stomach as he pulled down my pants. I wasn't wearing underwear, as we established earlier. Soon, we were both naked. He stood up and reached behind me with both arms and pulled me against his hard body. I reached for the sides of his waist and tickled him with the tips of my fingers. He bent down and picked me up carrying me toward the water. The sun was full and felt closer than normal, its warmth on my naked body. He gently lay me directly on the shore line and placed himself on top of me. I could feel his chest against mine and the beating of his heart. It felt natural being with him, but I still felt nervous around him. I was aroused but totally calm. He still had one arm around the small of my back holding me tightly against him. My back was arched, and my breasts were standing on their own from my arousal and the heat of the sun against the cool water. He started licking my nipples and sucking on them. I could feel the water trickling up between our legs. I rolled him over and moved down on him to take him in my mouth. I sucked and licked him as the water, coming in harder than before, kissed our bodies. He grabbed my head and pulled my mouth to his. His desire showed in everything he did. He shared so much passion with me that I was physically overwhelmed by his emotions. I felt sad for Rafael never having felt the things we'd shared. I wanted to make up for years of him not feeling love and passion and lust. I gave myself to him completely in every way.

We held each other, in between making love in every way on the shoreline, and then in the water. We felt each other's bodies and held onto the other's flesh, having sex and orgasms one after another.

Eventually we walked up to the beach hand-in-hand to where our clothes were scattered in the sand. We both laughed at the sight. Then we picked up our belongings and carried them back to the stairway up the ridge, though the garden, and then up the stairs to the deck. We dropped our things onto one of the many lounge chairs and walked into the villa.

I hadn't seen any of the bedrooms, so I just followed behind him and we went to the one facing the outside deck. A rush of wonderment filled me as we entered the room and saw the huge iron canopy bed with an intricately carved headboard standing prominently in the room. Layer upon layer of metallic peach fabric surrounded the four posts of the bed. The room was painted shades of peach and salmon with gorgeous bronze accents. I stood naked in the doorway, looking out the back doors that were open to the deck. I heard Rafael turn on the shower and walk back into the bedroom.

"What's going on in that head of yours?"

It had been hours and hours since any audible word had been spoken. I loved the silence between us. We never felt the need to ruin the moment with words. I turned around and smiled at him. I can only imagine what I looked like, because he looked exhausted.

"I'm feeling a little emotional and tired. Thank you for sharing all of this with me. Thank you for sharing yourself and your passion, but most of all, thank you for loving me."

"Come here," he said, his voice sounded raspy.

I walked to him and put my arms around his waist. He kissed me sweetly. He could kiss me into the next day. I got lost in his mouth every time he shared it with me. We walked to the shower and slipped in. I could feel the sun had also kissed me; the water stung just a little bit. As usual we used my Jasmine body wash and Pantene shampoo and conditioner. I loved the smell of Jasmine. I had Jasmine planted around my back porch at home, and the aromas that filled my backyard were always wonderful. We each lingered with some sensual kisses, then Rafael reached for a towel, handed it to me, and got one for himself. He wrapped it around his waist and walked into the living room after another kiss.

I stayed in the bathroom and blew dry my hair. It was easy. My hair was shoulder length, and had just a few wisps that fell around my eyes. I found all of the cosmetics that Kit had picked up for me, and it was like Christmas. Everything was the exact shades of make-up I wore. I put some tinted gloss on my lips to hide the slight swelling left by Rafael's soft sucking as well as the cut from the goon that was still healing. When I finished, I walked out of the bedroom out into the open living space and kitchen. Rafael was on his cell phone, but as he saw me walk out, he handed over a glass of sangria he made from the fresh fruits in the kitchen. Impressively, he even had chunks of the fruit in the glass with a slice of orange on the edge. I smiled as I planted a kiss on his cheek and took the glass. He made an annoyed face about the phone call, and I shook my head like it was fine.

I walked out to the lounge chairs on the deck, took off my towel and laid it on the chaise next to the table. The chair was already reclined at a perfect angle, and I lowered myself down softly and closed my eyes, enjoying the sun's rays and gentle breeze. Rafael walked out and joined me, laying his towel down and rolling on his side to look at me. There was that fantastic smile. I wondered if he was up to something. He held up his glass and said,

"To Spain."

I lifted my drink and touched it to his. Rafael's eyes were twinkling like the brightest stars on a perfectly clear night.

"To Spain," I said in return.

The sangria went down quickly, soothing the parched feeling after hours out in the sun and ocean. It was as easy to drink as fruit juice. Rafael walked inside to get the pitcher he made and refilled our glasses, then picked up my pack of cigarettes and slid a couple out of the pack. He lit them both and handed one to me. He didn't usually smoke with me, but I liked when he did.

"So how are you enjoying our honeymoon so far?" I asked.

"I still have at least three days of it left; I'll have to get back to you on that." He snickered, mocking me.

I loved the way he knew me so well in such a short time. He understood my sense of humor, which made it easy. He bantered back and forth with me, matched me jest for jest, and I ate it up. I put out my cigarette and excused myself to go to the bathroom and put some lotion on. When I came out, Rafael had turned on the stereo inside loud enough to hear it clearly out on the deck. He was standing against the deck railing looking out to the ocean. He looked so beautiful standing there. His tan lines were almost gone, and his skin glistened in the sun. I walked up behind him and he never heard me. He must have been deep in thought because when I put the palms of my hands against his back, he almost jumped.

"Take it easy big guy. You're not scared of little ole me are you?" I said. "Just relax, I promise I won't hurt you."

I started massaging his back and shoulders and then down to his lower back and butt. His body was the perfect mold of how a man should look. His legs were incredible, his thighs were huge, and his calves were awesome. They barely had any hair on them, and in fact he had very little hair on his body with the exception of his fabulous head of hair. His skin was hot from the sun, and touching him gave me a glorious sensation. I pictured him as the perfect underwear model. He turned around to face me and I asked him,

"What were you thinking about?"

"The tango," he said, but I knew there was something else on his mind.

He took my hands in his and started showing me the basic steps while following the rhythm of the music. I picked it up quickly, somehow remembering the easy parts I rehearsed for my wedding years ago. The intricate steps were a bit harder to remember, but it was easy to follow along with Rafael leading. With my leg placed between his, I felt his erection rubbing against me as we turned. I held my composure and continued dancing the steps and feeling him rub against me every time we were close. He started laughing and I joined him. This was better than any dance class I'd ever had. Naked, dancing a naughty version of the tango outside in plain sight, and not giving it a second thought. Definitely not part of my normal daily routine. Normal would be dancing around the kitchen in my pajamas to the theme song to Sponge Bob while doing the dishes.

18
Chapter

We took a break from the dancing. Listening to the music on the radio and sipping our drinks, we sat next to each other on one chaise. I set my drink down and leaned my head against his shoulder. He set his glass down and lay against the chaise, and I curled up behind him. I kissed his neck and wrapped my arm around his waist feeling his belly button. We just lay there for a while, and then he rolled onto his back and looked at me. He grabbed my waist and pulled one of my legs over his thigh.

"How is it that in fifteen years in this profession, you are the only one that has ever made me feel safe?"

"It's probably the protective mom in me." I smiled at him and he put his hand on the side of my neck and pulled my mouth to his.

By now I could feel how wet I was rubbing myself against his hip. I was touching his chest and pinching his nipples between my fingers. I could feel his erection tickling the back of my leg. It felt so good just kissing and touching each other as the sun began sinking into the horizon. This felt like such a long day to me and it wasn't even over. Rafael moved onto his side slipping his thigh between my legs. I felt his erection tease my opening before entering a little at a time. His whole groin was rubbing between my legs, and within minutes I was ready to come. I tried to hold it and concentrate on Rafael but that didn't work.

"Ah mi Dios que usted se siente tan bueno." I whispered in his ear, "Oh my God you feel so good." I moaned and purred and felt Rafael hitting deeper inside me until I felt him give in to the pleasure of our bodies. He slowed down and when he could find his breath again, he said,

"I see what you mean about the whispering in the ear." Rafael let all his muscles relax, pulled out of me, and lay on his back while closing his eyes. He looked peaceful and beautiful and tired. The sun was close to setting and I didn't want to miss it, not from where I was laying. I thought Rafael had dozed off for a few minutes, but I woke him when the sun was about to bid adieu, and we watched it until all that was left was the bright, sensual colors reflecting off the water. Of course it would be more sensual, considering our current state of lying naked on a balcony overlooking the sea in Spain, still feeling euphoric from our orgasms.

"I agree the sunsets are more sensual here. Thank you for letting me make that determination on my own." I kissed his lips and sucked on the bottom one gently. It was starting to get cooler without the sun, so he got up and gently pulled me with him. We walked in and went into the bedroom. Rafael collapsed on the bed and I laughed. I could see that he was smiling.

"Why don't you lie down for a while, and I'll go take a hot bath if you don't mind."

I walked to the other side of the bed and covered him up, and he was already asleep. I kissed his face and walked to the bathroom. I started the water and went to get another glass of Sangria. I could feel the sand on the marble floor and the scent of the beach. The ocean and the flowers from the gardens outside permeated the room. It was perfect. I headed back to the deck with my Sangria and smoked a little of one of the hand rolled cigarettes while the tub was filling. I went inside and slid in the bath. I soaked and felt how my skin was still so soft considering I waxed six days ago. I could hear Rafael snoring quietly, which seemed rather cute. He was so sensual and sexy I could hardly stand to be away from him. I let the water out of the tub and dried myself.

I went to the kitchen and put away all the food, then returned to the bedroom and I crawled in bed next to him and held him. He woke up several times through the night and we made love again and again, quietly seducing each other, sleeping in between.

I heard a noise in the kitchen and sat up. Rafael was still sound asleep. Great ears for a special agent. I grabbed my robe and walked to the door of the bedroom and peeked around the corner. I saw Rafael's team in the kitchen making breakfast and coffee. I didn't even realize that it was light out. Rock saw me from the bedroom door and smiled at me. I smiled in return and said,

"Beunos dias," smiling at each of them, as they laughed again at the thought that I spoke Spanish and never told anyone.

They said good morning in unison, and I noticed they had brought all the food. As if I had walked away, they all went back to their discussions and tasks. I closed the bedroom door and walked back to Rafael still asleep. His face looked so sweet and innocent. I rubbed my nose against his, and he jumped up like I scared him to death. I just stood there looking at him like he was crazy and started to laugh.

"Good morning, Mr. Montoya." I was still giggling, "I'm sorry; I should know better than to sneak up on you."

He grabbed me from the side of the bed and pulled me on top of him. He reached for my hips and moved me up on him. I kissed him and whispered in his ear,

"Your team is in the kitchen making breakfast." I pulled away to look in his eyes.

"Then we'll be ready just in time." He smiled and lifted his mouth to reach mine. He untied my robe and with one pull from the back he had it on the floor. We were on top of the covers, and then he rolled me over and tucked me under him as he kissed me. He whispered in my ear in Spanish that he wanted me for breakfast, and I reached to hold his back. He parted my legs and moved slowly between them while he was softly touching my breasts. He moved to my neck then to my lips. His erection found where it wanted to go and slid, as slowly as he kissed me, inside of me. There was no tension in this room. It was erotic and sexy and felt so amazing.

It made me think of Matt again. We had this fire when we first starting dating. I remember saying to him in the beginning that I couldn't imagine going a day without making love to him. It was always exciting and sexual. Things change, like having a baby. Neither of us ever had enough energy to even agree to a quickie. Now, perhaps because I was hitting my sexual prime, going on forty, I wanted more. We'd changed sexually from the beginning, but it was almost better where we were now. Knowing what the other liked, how to satisfy each other to the fullest, and comfortable enough with each other to try new things. I'd also been reading some very erotic romance novels lately. The problem was that I could count on one hand how many times a year Matt and I had sex. He just didn't want me like he used to.

As my mind continued to wander, so did Rafael. He moved down and licked me from my navel down. His tongue was such a tease, and I loved it. He rolled me over and took me from behind.

His mouth was on my shoulders, his hand touching me between my legs, softly rubbing me. That always did it for me. I was overcome by the physical part of letting go and feeling Rafael enjoying me at the same time, letting go himself. We fell flat on the bed, Rafael pushed the hair from the side of my face, kissed my neck and ears, and then turned on his side and fell next to me on the bed. He looked into my eyes, and he looked sad again.

"What is it?" I asked.

"It's not going to be easy to let you go." He kissed me.

"Rafael, I love you. I love the things we've shared, and you will always be a part of me." I kissed him. "Besides, after a few more days you might just be sick of me and happy to get rid of me." I laughed because it was possible.

"I doubt that. I guess we should get some breakfast." We cleaned up in the bathroom and I put on my robe.

For the first time since I'd been here, I walked into the closet and couldn't believe my eyes. It was full of the most gorgeous clothes I'd ever seen. From formal to beach attire, every outfit was lined up with all the right accessories and shoes and jewelry. I was in heaven. Rafael was just wearing a pair of pants when he left the bedroom, and I asked him to send Kit in. He smiled when he realized what I was doing in the closet and nodded happily.

Kit came in the bedroom and to the closet with a huge grin on her face, and I started laughing.

"Kit, I can't believe you did all this. I wish my closet at home looked like this. Thank you."

I hugged her and she was so excited to show me everything she had bought, including the gown and jewels for this evening's event. I had never seen a gown like that one in all my life. It was the color of metallic cinnamon that looked different in the lighting. It was a floor length silk gown with a beautiful pattern from the shoulder, across the bodice, and down the right side to the slit, then followed around the bottom, all in tiny beads of golden colors. Shoes to match and jewelry fit for a princess. I just hoped it fit.

"Try it on." Kit said smiling.

I did and the mirrors in the bathroom gave me a view from every angle. I did feel like a princess. How cliché. But it was true. The gown was amazing on me, and I opened the door to show Kit. I lifted my eyebrows like 'what do you think' and her face said it all.

"I knew it would be perfect. You look stunning."

"I love it, thank you so much." I hugged her again.

"Now take it off before Rafael comes in looking for you."

Kit smiled and walked out of the bedroom closing the door behind her. I closed the door to the bathroom and took the gown off, hung it back up, and took it back to the closet. I picked a tank top and a pair of capri pants and got dressed. I walked out to the open room and they were all standing in the kitchen talking. Rafael saw me walk toward him, and he poured me a cup of coffee.

"Good morning Mrs. Montoya." Rafael kissed me and handed me the mug.

I just smiled at him and turned around to see what everyone was up to. Breakfast looked like it had been ready for a while, so I grabbed a plate and helped myself. They all followed my lead. We all brought our plates out to the deck and sat around the table. I was enjoying all of them in their own conversations while laughing with each other. It was nice to see everyone happy and ready for the day. I looked at Rafael and he was looking at me smiling. He looked really rested and happy.

"You are most entertaining when you think to yourself." Rafael prodded.

"Maybe I should start charging for the entertainment." I smiled back and everyone was smiling at the two of us. I knew I made faces and talked with my hands, even when I was just thinking something in my head. It probably was entertaining.

We all ate, then cleaned up in the kitchen. Everyone sat at the dining room table and waited for Rafael to start talking. Ready for business, I was guessing. He spoke in English when he started, but about halfway through his directions to the team, he continued in Spanish and raised his voice like he was worried and scared. I listened to everything they talked about and knew where everyone was going to be at tonight's event. Many of the local agents would be undercover as security, Kit and Rock would be guests also, and some would be on the staff as servers. I started to feel nervous all of a sudden, and my face must have shown it. I looked around the table at all these people and then to Rafael. He saw my expression and asked,

"Is something wrong? Maya, are you okay?"

"Um, no nothing is wrong. I'm fine," I lied. I could feel every part of my insides shaking and trembling. I was surprised I was so calm on the outside. I wasn't paying much attention to the rest of the discussion. My mind just wondered in a million directions, and I needed to have a cigarette.

"Please excuse me for a moment." I stood up and went outside. I was hoping I wasn't making a big deal by leaving, but I just needed to get some air. I lit a cigarette and walked to the railing and sat on the first step down to the gardens. I could feel myself relaxing almost instantly. I just sat there for at least a half hour.

I heard Rafael call my name, and as I turned around, he saw where I was sitting and came over to me. He sat next to me and looked me in the eyes,

"You don't have to do this."

"I won't lie, I'm a little anxious. I'll be fine when the time comes. I'm usually very calm in stressful situations."

"I'll be at your side the entire time." He lifted my chin and looked at me with a serious face, "I won't let anything happen to you."

"I know."

We just sat for a while looking at the view. It was very beautiful there. I'd never forget this picture in my head. The flowers, the cliffs and the ocean. It would be forever imprinted in my heart. I'd make it my happy place from now on during those times I wished I was somewhere else.

"Has everyone left?" I asked.

"Yes, they wanted to give us some time alone before we have to get ready. They are all excited to see you tonight."

I smiled thinking of the gown. I was feeling better and asked,

"Do you want to go for a walk?"

"I'd go anywhere with you." He stood and took my hand.

We walked down to the beach and along the shore. He had his arms around me walking next to me; he was so warm. It's not that it was cool outside; he just seemed to always make me feel warm all over. We walked a good distance, and Rafael stopped walking and turned me to face him. He touched my face with his fingers and leaned in to touch his lips to mine. I grabbed his waist and pulled myself closer to him, feeling his chest, and then his muscular back. His skin felt like it was on fire. His touch made mine feel the same. He just kissed me and touched the skin on my neck and shoulders. Kissing him was pure bliss. I was so turned on, but I wanted to wait until after tonight.

"What time is it?" I asked him.

"It is almost one o'clock in the afternoon. We have a car picking us up at five this evening."

"We should walk back," I said as I looked at how far we had gotten.

I put my arm around his waist, and his arm was around my shoulder as we walked back to the villa. Rafael was as quiet as I was. I wondered what he was thinking about. I'm sure his mind was completely full with the mission tonight. He was team leader, overseeing all the agents from various agencies, and he even had local authorities waiting in the wings. I was sure everything would be okay. I had to believe that. We reached the stairs and walked up toward the deck.

19
Chapter

I wanted to lay naked outside and enjoy gorgeous weather and privacy. I stopped at the lounge chair and took my clothes off. Rafael stood there watching me. I lay down on the chaise and looked up to Rafael.

"Lie down, relax with me." I smiled innocently.

"And how do you expect me to relax with you lying next to me like that?" He raised his eyebrows and pointed his arms at me.

"Mr. Montoya, you need to focus on tonight and relax. So sit down and be quiet." I started to laugh and he just shook his head and lay down on the chaise next to me. Then I added,

"Besides, I want to flirt with you all day until the anticipation is too much to wait any longer. You had me for breakfast, now you'll have to wait for dessert tonight." His face was pathetic, and then he looked at me with begging eyes. The front of his pants was tented from his erection. I leaned over and kissed him, wanting him, but then I just leaned my head back on the chaise, closed my eyes and felt the sun on my body. I was aroused from the sheer fact I was laying here naked in the sun. I looked over at Rafael, and he still had his eyes closed and was very quiet. He looked so relaxed, and I was feeling better knowing that he wasn't very concerned about the job we had to do tonight. He opened his eyes and looked at me and found me looking at him. He asked,

"Do we have any sangria left?"

"The rest of the pitcher is in the refrigerator," I answered.

"Would you like some?" he asked as he stood up.

"I would love some, extra fruit in mine please." I grinned and added, "Gracias, me amore."

He headed for the kitchen, and I heard his cell phone ring. He talked for several minutes with a serious tone and then came out with a tray holding the sangria, two glasses, and some fruit from breakfast.

"Is everything okay?" I asked knowing something was going on.

"One of the agents working security for the event tonight just called in that they brought in more security at the last minute. I'm sure it's just precautionary." He was avoiding my eyes and pouring the sangria into our glasses. Rafael handed me one and looked at me holding his glass up.

"Until tonight," Rafael said with a pouting face that he would have to wait until tonight to make love to me again.

I toasted to that and took a sip from the glass. It was so cold from being in the refrigerator. I pulled a piece of pineapple out of my drink and rubbed it over my nipple. It felt so cold. The juice from the fruit and the drink dripped down the side of my breast. Rafael was at my side licking the juice from my breast, and then I fed him the piece of pineapple. He lay back down on his chaise and closed his eyes again. The tent in his pants remained. I started to think about tonight. I wondered why I felt Rafael wasn't telling me something from that phone call. I looked back at him and said,

"If I'm going to trust you, you have to trust me."

"What are you talking about?" He asked.

"What are you not telling me?"

"We don't know yet. We got a lead that there was a hit on the guy we are going after tonight. His name is Luis Sanchez, and he apparently has pissed off a lot of people and many of them would like to see him dead. They'll call me when there is more information; for now, we go on as planned."

"Okay then." I smiled at him.

"Come over here," he said quietly.

I stood up and put one leg over the side of his chair and sat on his lap not facing him. I was still holding my glass and laid my back against his chest so my front was still getting the sun. I let my head fall back to rest against his shoulder, and I felt his arm come around my side and touch my skin. I could feel his erection between my butt cheeks. When I clenched them, he moaned and whispered in my ear in Spanish that I was torturing him. I giggled and unclenched. Rafael put his chin against my forehead, and we both just closed our eyes and enjoyed the peace and quiet. I lifted my neck up to take a taste of my drink and asked, "Sip?"

I turned around on top of him so that I was facing him and tortured him some more with my position. I tilted the glass to his lips and he drank. I picked another piece of fruit from my drink and put it in my mouth. I leaned in toward him and shared the fruit with his mouth. I kissed him softly, our tongues playing back and forth with the fruit. When it was gone, I sucked on his bottom lip and then licked his mouth. He was groaning in pain, and I was going to leave a wet spot on his pants for sure. I was also having a hard time controlling myself. I got up and returned to my own chaise. The tension was building so quickly I wasn't sure I could wait until dessert, but I wanted to long for him all day, until the passion was so intense I could hardly stand it. It was an incredible turn on.

Just then his phone rang again. It was probably a good thing to take our minds off each other. He went inside to take the call. I stayed right where I was and just let all my feelings get swept away in the breeze. I felt calm. In stressful situations at home it would be me telling Hayden to be brave and strong and that he was a big boy. I was always surprised by his courage. He was very shy and when he went off on his own to do something, I was always so proud of him. I still had a hard time with the thought of him going to kindergarten next fall. I was going to have to learn to be brave too.

Matt and I had talked about what I wanted to do when Hayden went to school, because I was going to have to find something to fill up those empty days. Some of the books I had read lately made me want to go into private investigations. I followed a friend's husband a couple of times, and it was really exciting to me. I researched becoming one and all the different fields involved. Matt thought I would love doing something like that. I had this great sense of detail. He actually moved things in the house to see how long it would take me to notice. We'd see when the time came, but for now I was going to enjoy Hayden everyday he was home with me. For this, I felt very fortunate. I appreciated how hard Matt worked so we didn't have to worry.

Rafael walked back outside and sat on the end of my chaise. He looked nervous. He reached for my cigarette pack and pulled out two. I remembered the last time he did that before he had to tell me something. I felt my stomach tighten and I waited for him. He handed me a cigarette and he smoked his for a minute before he finally said,

"There has been a change of plans. You are going to stay here. The danger is too high now; I can't risk something happening to you. I will explain that you were not feeling well, and send them your regards. I'll leave you this phone so that we can reach each other." He looked at me very seriously and waited for me to say something.

"No," I simply stated. "I can't protect you from here." I tried to make him laugh, but it didn't work.

"Maya, I can't let you do this." He was shaking his head, looking down to the deck floor.

"You don't have a choice, so I suggest you tell me what I need to know." My look was calm but serious.

"Promise me that you will not leave my side. I don't care if you have to use the bathroom, I will be going with you."

"I promise." I reached for his hand and he looked up to meet my eyes.

"We've been told to stand down on our orders. There are many hits on Luis' life tonight, and there could be bullets flying in every direction. It would be better if it weren't us taking him out. We can only find out what will happen as it happens and that's really risky."

"So be on the lookout for people who are carrying guns, play the part of a new bride deeply in love, and be home before midnight. Got it!" I grinned and he finally got a chuckle in before his phone rang again. He answered it while still sitting at my feet. The person on the other end did all the talking and then he disconnected the call. I waited again.

"I have to go. There is an agent outside the front door. I'll get ready with my team and pick you up at five o'clock."

"Don't be late!" I sat up and he grabbed me around the waist and pulled me against him. He kissed me so hard and then pulled his face away enough to look me in the eyes. He didn't need to say anything, I felt what he felt. He went into the bedroom and retrieved his tuxedo and shoes, and I walked toward where he stood just inside the open door wall to the deck. I kissed his neck and brushed my lips against his, just to gently touch them, and pulled away. We both smiled at each other, and he turned and walked to the front entrance.

Everything was going to be fine. I had plenty of time to get ready. I liked spending hours getting ready for something big. At home I had about five minutes to put make-up on, or Hayden would take my powder brushes and start cleaning my vanity with them. I was looking forward to a few hours of primping. It wasn't until I went to take a sip of my sangria that I realized my hand was shaking. Crap! I went for the hand rolled cigarette and smoked just enough to calm my nerves.

I walked into the bedroom from the outside and to the bathroom. I started the water and poured in the jasmine bubble bath. I refilled my drink and went back into the bathroom. I set my glass down on the counter and looked at myself in the mirror. I actually felt as beautiful on the outside as I did on the inside. There had always been periods of my life when I felt one or the other, but never both at once. Before I had Hayden, I felt beautiful on the outside. He made me feel beautiful on the inside, but I lost the beauty I felt toward myself on the outside. Matt always told me how beautiful I was, but sometimes I let things go while staying at home. Some days, I wore my pajamas all day long and never got dressed at all.

I looked at my breasts in the mirror and was still impressed. I had two breast augmentations in my twenties. Had I known my mother would die of breast cancer, I don't think I would have been so vain. Regardless, they looked good. I never produced enough milk when Hayden was born, so they were never swollen or full. It was fine with me because the first time they put Hayden to my nipple, I wanted to go through the roof. Something people don't tell you beforehand is that breast feeding hurts like hell

I took my glass to the edge of the tub, climbed in and settled back. It was perfect, not hot, just warm and relaxing. I reached for the razor in the basket in the corner of the tub and shaved everything, just in case stubble was coming in. I wanted to make sure my skin was as soft and smooth as possible. I got out and dried myself off. I saw some lotion sitting on the counter and put it all over my body. It smelled so clean and it made my skin glisten with little shimmers of gold. I looked radiant. I put on my silk nightgown that went with the robe I had worn earlier and went out on the deck. You could feel the sun getting weaker and farther away. I sat at one of the tables with an umbrella and had a cigarette and sipped my sangria. I still couldn't get over the view from this villa. Maybe tonight I would get to see more of Spain, although, I had a feeling that I was going to see more than I wanted to.

I went back inside and put my hair up in rollers and put my make-up on, taking my time. It was amazing how much easier it was to put on eyeliner without Hayden fighting me to see himself in my magnifying mirror on my vanity table.

I went into the kitchen and found some bottled water, took it to the lavish living room, and sat on the couch admiring all the elegant furnishings. The villa looked like a model home, everything perfectly placed. Large oversized furniture took up most of the open room. There were palm trees inside and plants everywhere. Every doorway had high archways. I guess it was what I would imagine it would be in Spain. It was still hard to digest all the things that had happened so far that week. I wasn't ready to go home. Not quite yet.

I noticed a pad of paper on the kitchen counter and got up to see if there was anything written on it. The top page was torn off, but I could see the imprint from the writing pressed into the paper from Rafael writing hard. I held it sideways and could read what was written. Luis Sanchez was underlined. Interesting.

I went to the laptop that was still lying on the dining room table and opened it. I did a search for Mr. Sanchez, and all kinds of results popped up. Owning property and businesses all over this town, he was sure to be a popular subject. There was one article that was a personal interview and I clicked on it. He was actually very good looking and not at all how I imagined. He looked in his forties but he was actually fifty eight. He had been arrested several times; it seemed there was always someone trying to take him down. He had a wife and two daughters, who seemed to be active in the community. There were a lot of scandals and accusations of affairs. I kind of expected more information, but at least now I knew some things about him. I closed the laptop and walked into the bathroom.

I took the curlers out of my hair and sprayed it with hairspray upside down. I pulled sections of my hair away from my face with little jeweled pins, leaving a few stray curls around my face. I put on the jewelry and adjusted my hair to see the earrings better. The necklace was rows of gorgeous metallic beads with one brown topaz stone that hung from the center. I really was starting to feel like Cinderella.

I took a break and sat outside for a little while. All I had left to do was put on the dress and shoes. I didn't know what time it was, but I was relaxed and was enjoying the quiet. My anticipation had been building all day. I couldn't wait to see Rafael, though seeing him might just put me over the edge. I sipped on the water I had been carrying around from earlier and smoked the rest of the hand rolled cigarette. I sat outside a little longer before I went in to put on my dress. I pulled it out of the closet and took it to the bathroom and hung it up. The shoes were just a shade darker than the dress, but they were beaded in the same colors and had to have been made for this dress. I couldn't wear a bra because it only had one shoulder, but thank God Kit bought some lacy panties because I was going to need them tonight, if only to contain myself. I put on the sheer lace panties and reached for the gown. I still couldn't believe how breathtaking it was, and it fit me like it was made just for me. It was probably a good thing I burned some extra calories that week or it might not have fit me so well. I was sure that I had lost several pounds in the last six days. I took a deep breath, looked myself over, and I grinned like a teenaged girl going to her first prom. I freshened up my make-up and grabbed the clutch purse that went with the dress. I opened it and inside was a cigarette case. It was silver, embossed and antiqued. The pattern was of two lovers on the shore. It took my breath away. Inside there were six cigarettes. I thought to myself that six wasn't going to be enough. Not for tonight. I put the cell phone inside my purse and noticed from the time on the phone I had twenty minutes. I had everything and went outside and stood against the railing and looked out to the ocean. This must be a dream. When I thought about being here with Rafael, it didn't seem real. I had no idea how everything was going to play out tonight. I didn't know what to expect at all. Maybe that's why I seemed so calm right now; I didn't know what to be afraid of.

20
Chapter

A loud knocking came from the door and I froze. I was quiet for a few moments and then a second knocking. I walked toward the front of the villa and opened the door. A man dressed in a black suit was standing alone.

"I'm here to take you to Mr. Montoya," he said politely.

I wondered where the agent was that was supposed to be here. I then wondered why Rafael didn't call me if the plans had changed. I knew immediately that this was all wrong. I had to play along. I knew that Rafael would know what was happening and find me.

"I'm ready." I smiled at him, hoping I didn't look as nervous as I felt.

He walked me to the car and opened the back door of a very nice silver Mercedes. I slipped in and he closed the door. As he walked around to the other side of the car, I opened my purse and pushed the send button on the phone, then took out my compact mirror and applied more lip gloss. When he got in and started the car I asked him,

"Where is my husband?"

"He asked me to bring you to the estate where the party is and said he would meet you there." He peeked at me in the rear view mirror. I smiled at him and he returned the smile. Did he think I was stupid? I wondered if I hadn't read all the detective and mystery books I had recently, if I would have noticed these things.

"And where is it that we are going now?" I asked.

"Mr. Sanchez would like a word with you." He looked at me again in the mirror.

"Where?" I was getting irritated.

"Mr. Sanchez would like to speak to you at his home," he replied.

"Then we will be joining the others at the party?" I asked.

"Yes, Senora Montoya."

I pushed the disconnect button on my phone in case someone wanted to look in my purse. As we drove, I looked out the window trying to notice anything and everything, not that I would know where I was, but I could describe the things I saw. After fifteen minutes or so we reached the gated entrance to his home, and I wondered what Mr. Sanchez wanted to talk to me about.

The mansion left me speechless. The drive pulled up into a roundabout with a large fountain in the middle. All the gorgeous arched windows in the front of the home faced that circle drive. I was so out of my mind with fear and couldn't imagine why this man wanted to see me. I tried to remain calm as the driver got out and came around to open my door. He held out his hand to help me, and I took it and stepped out of the car. He put my hand under his arm and walked me up about ten stairs to the main door. The door opened as we reached the top, and the driver introduced me to the man that opened the door, who obviously worked security for Mr. Sanchez. He then invited me inside and I followed him to this breathtaking veranda outside. Lush plants and flowers surrounded the round shaped patio overlooking the ocean.

"Ah, Mrs. Montoya, I've been expecting you." A voice echoed from across the lengthy patio. He spoke in English with a very strong accent. Then he added,

"Mr. Montoya is very lucky man; you are quite a stunning woman."

As I walked closer, I recognized him from the computer articles I read earlier and the accompanying photos. He was tall and slender, salt and pepper hair cut short, and dressed in a black tuxedo. He reached for my hand and kissed it. He pulled out a cigar and asked,

"Do you mind if I smoke?"

"Not at all, if I may join you." I smiled at him. He was very charming.

"You smoke cigars?" he asked, with a questioning face.

"Only when I am drinking or golfing." I laughed shyly.

"What shall we drink then?" he asked.

"Rob Roy straight up, thank you." I was amazed at how well he spoke English, and then I wondered if he even knew what a Rob Roy was. He nodded his head and smiled as he turned and walked to the outside bar. He returned and handed me a glass, then pulled two cigars out of his pocket, cut the ends off, and handed me one. I put it up to my nose and closed my eyes. It was a Savor Macanudo, 1968. This was definitely not like the cigars I smoked at home; these were a little out of my price range. I thought of my neighbor, Gero, who would love one of these. We often sat around the pool with a drink and a cigar. He appreciated the good things in life.

Mr. Sanchez led me to a table and pulled a chair out for me. I put my bag on the table then my drink. I put the cigar in my mouth and he leaned in to light it. I waited until he lit his.

"Thank you, this is really quite wonderful. Was there something you wanted to talk to me about, Mr. Sanchez?" I looked directly at him and puffed on my cigar.

"Please call me Luis," he said softly. "My wife was sorry that she could not be here to meet you. It seems you have a lot in common with all the work you both do for the children. She was wondering how long you were going to be here in Spain," he said smiling.

"Luis, obviously you have been watching me and knew I was alone when you sent for me. This is a conversation you could have had with me at the party, when my husband was with me. Is there something else you have on your mind?" I stared him in the eye and showed very little emotion. Luis smiled and answered,

"You are not only beautiful but smart. I like you Mrs. Montoya, which is why I can't let you go to the party tonight. I know that tonight may be my last hours. It will not be safe for you."

"What are you saying Luis, how do you know what will happen tonight?" I remained unemotional.

"I've sent my family away. I am asking you for a favor." He pulled an envelope from the inside of his tuxedo jacket and handed it to me. There was no writing on it and it was sealed. He continued, "Will you give this to my wife if something happens to me tonight?" He looked genuinely sad.

"Why have you been watching us, and what do you know about me that would make you want to save me." I sipped my drink and waited for him to answer.

"I know your husband, Mrs. Montoya, and this is not your war. You shouldn't be here."

Obviously there were things way over my head going on here, so I had to play my cards quickly. Instantly, I decided the only thing I could do was feel bad for him. I reached for his hand and said,

"My name is Angel."

"Angel then, do you think I am a bad man?" He was feeling guilty and was looking for some forgiveness that wasn't mine to give.

"Luis, even the best of men are misunderstood sometimes." I raised my eyebrow and smiled warmly at him.

"I would be happy to give this to your wife if something happens, highly unlikely as it seems, but I think we need to get out and really enjoy this evening. Shall we? If something happens to any of us tonight, we should go out happy." I broke away from his gaze and put the envelope in my purse. I didn't know what was going to happen tonight, but I didn't intend on getting killed or anything else my imagination could conjure up.

I asked him to dance with me and he looked confused. I took his hand and we stood together next to the table in an open space. I told him to close his eyes and remember a time he danced with his wife. I told him to feel the music and the passion. He started swaying with me slowly until I could tell he was remembering a particular moment. I closed my eyes and enjoyed the moment as well. He was a really good dancer and it was easy to follow along with him. He held me close to him and after several minutes, I put my head against his shoulder. I could tell that he was a romantic person and loved his wife and family dearly. The song in his head must have ended. He stopped dancing and opened his eyes. I looked at him, and his eyes were brimming with tears. He held my hands in his and said,

"Thank you."

I nodded my head as I looked to the floor. It was hard to imagine what he must be feeling right now thinking that he was going to be killed tonight. Words wouldn't have been enough. I kissed him on each cheek and stepped back.

"Shall we join the party?" I smiled and continued, "My husband must be worried sick."

We walked inside the house and his men were all waiting. Luis nodded to them, and we all proceeded to the front door and down the steps to the cars waiting. Luis and I got into the back seat of the second car, and they both pulled away down the long drive to the gate. Not one person spoke a word the entire ride there. We rode for about fifteen minutes and pulled up to another gate, and the front car checked in and both cars were let inside. There was an even longer driveway up to the mansion with cars parked all along one side of the drive. Our car pulled up to the entrance to let us out.

"I don't know how to thank you; you are an Angel, Mrs. Montoya. I will make sure I compliment your husband for his excellent taste in women." Luis nodded to me in a heartfelt way.

"It has been my pleasure. Now let's go dance the night away. Shall we Mr. Sanchez?" I winked at him.

He opened the door and reached his hand out for mine to help me out of the car. He tucked my arm under his and looked at me. The two front entrance doors were opened for us, and I saw Rafael standing right inside the entry. He walked toward us and we met together just inside the door.

"My apologies Mr. Montoya for keeping your new bride from you. She is an extraordinary woman. Again, I'm sorry. I will leave you now. Enjoy your evening."

He shook hands with Rafael and smiled at me before he turned around and walked away. Rafael took my hand and led me to a room off the entry. He turned to look at me, grabbed me by the shoulders, pulled me hard into his body, and kissed me, needy and wanting. I remembered the anticipation the moment his lips touched mine. I pulled my face away just enough to look into his eyes.

"I'm okay. I'm sorry if you've been worried." I felt bad for what he must have been going through. I knew how I would have felt if it were him.

"Thank you for the heads up call. We had your dress wired and a tracking device put in the hem of the shoulder. We heard everything and I wasn't worried a bit." He shook his head and took my hands in his. "You look ravishing. There are no words to describe the feeling I had when I saw you walk up the stairs to the front doors." He pulled me into him again, and with an almost painful look on his face, put his mouth to mine. I closed my eyes and felt what he felt in the way that he kissed me. I broke away and asked him,

"Shall we join the party, Mr. Montoya?" I smiled confidently, he put his hand on the small of my back, and we walked into the main room full of people.

I was astounded. I scanned the room, taking note of people mingling, engaged in laughter and storytelling. There had to be at least one hundred people in this enormous main room. Everyone looked very happy, I thought, knowing that danger was lurking, it all seemed so ironic. It would really be a shame if something bad happened tonight. For now, I was living in the moment. That's all I could do. I saw everyone from Rafael's team at their designated stations. I smiled at Kit as Rafael and I went to one of the bars set up around the mansion. We ordered some wine and moved away to a quiet place.

"Mr. Montoya, seeing you in that tuxedo makes it very hard to control myself. I'm afraid I may not make it until dessert," I said staring at him over my glass as I took a sip.

"You handled the situation with Mr. Sanchez like a professional. We listened in awe when you danced with him. You are truly an amazing woman, although I have to say I wanted to kill the man myself for taking you. When you leave I'm going to have to retrain my team. You've made them all softies." He said, while letting out a cheerful laugh. I loved when he laughed, and I smirked at him and then whispered into his ear,

"And how about you Rafael, have you turned soft too?"

I looked at him seriously.

"Soft is not the word I would use, let's just say I'm happy I went with the longer coat tonight." He grinned provocatively. It was hard not to smile back at him when he looked like that.

"Rafael, what would you be doing right now if you knew that you may die tonight?" I looked at him with a questioning face.

"I'd be right here with you." He kissed me and didn't ask me that question in return. I was glad, because I would have had to say that I would want to go home. That's probably why he didn't ask me. He knew what I would say.

"Would you like to go outside on the veranda? I'd love to see what the view looks like from here." I really needed to sit and calm my nerves from my visit with Mr. Sanchez.

He nodded and we walked out to the circular veranda. It was similar to Luis' but much larger.

We sat at one of the couches grouped together. There were candles everywhere lighting the different seating areas sending out scents of vanilla in the light breeze. The veranda was very inviting, lush with plants and colorful pots of hanging flowers. I pulled out the cigarette case and looked at Rafael.

"Do you like it? I had it made for you." He gave me that sneaky smile.

"It's so beautiful, thank you, I love it." I leaned closer and kissed him, thanking him with my lips.

I took out two cigarettes and handed one to him. I had noticed earlier that there was no lighter in my purse. Rafael pulled one out of his pocket and lit my cigarette and then his, then returned it to his pocket. Our legs were touching each other as we sat on the outdoor couch. As I sat with my legs crossed, almost my entire right leg was exposed from the slit up the front of the dress.

"Has anything been going on here?" I asked.

"Right now we're just keeping tabs on the security and our eyes on the guests. Nothing unusual so far."

We sat until we finished our cigarettes and our wine and then decided we should be inside. I followed him, holding his hand as he walked in front of me leading the way. We stopped at one of the tables, and he put my purse down and signaled to the wait staff for more wine. He led me to the dance floor and faced me. We started to dance, warming up our bodies, briefly touching each other. It wasn't the tango, but it was even sexier the way he was moving me around right now. It was so sensual. The music was not fast, but not slow. It was just perfect for me to keep up with him whisking me around him.

"I want you," I whispered into his ear. Then suddenly, a quick flash in my peripheral view caught my eye, and I quickly glanced over to see a silver object under a man's jacket. He was standing against the wall in conversation with a few other men, then he twisted to the side and the object slid into hiding.

"I think I saw a gun under a man's jacket," I said after pausing a few seconds to collect myself and continue dancing.

"Who was it?"

I described him to Rafael. He leaned into me to look like he was kissing me, but asked into his tiny microphone if someone listening had a visual on the man. He said to find out who he was. I wasn't able to hear the other side of the conversation, only what Rafael was saying.

"My team may need to use some of their selective hearing skills for a little while." He laughed and then whispered in my ear.

"You have no idea how badly I want you right now. We may need to find a private bathroom soon." He kissed my neck and then began kissing my lips, gently touching them and holding his lips lightly against mine. I could feel his breath, the heat from it, against my mouth. Only our hands were touching and our lips. He moved his arm with his hand still holding mine to the small of my back and pulled me in closer. His kisses were getting a little harder, and I could feel how much he wanted me by his erection against me. Our dancing slowed down even though the music was faster on the crowded dance floor. It was like no one else in the world existed except for Rafael and me. He broke away to look at me and looked to the left.

"Copy," Rafael said and looked back to me again.

"What is it?"

"We are running facial recognition scans on the guests, and there was a match to a known business partner of Mr. Sanchez." He looked at me like it was no big deal.

"By the way, Mr. Sanchez said that he knew you, and this was not your war. Do you know anything about that?" I asked him. He really looked like he didn't know what I was talking about. He spoke to his team through his wire, and said, "Call Langley and get everyone doing backgrounds on Mr. Sanchez, going back several generations. Cross reference with any of my family. Thanks guys."

He returned his gaze to me,

"Shall we find a bathroom?"

"Rafael, dessert, remember?" I knew I was torturing myself as well as him. I still wanted to build the anticipation. We had only been here an hour-and-a-half, maybe. I couldn't cave now.

Besides I really wanted to see what was going on and what was going to happen. It was like leaving before the ending of a movie and never knowing what happened.

"Then maybe we should be having dinner at least." He stopped dancing and just kissed me.

He led me to the table where he had put my purse down and seated me. He moved his chair so that we were sitting next to each other and could both see most of the room. There were already two glasses of red wine waiting when we got to the table. We both reached for a glass and I held up my glass to him and toasted,

"To living in the moment." We touched each other's glass and sipped from the goblets. A waitress came over and gave us some menus for the dinner, just a few choices. With this many people it would be hard to have a full menu. I wasn't really hungry and just ordered a salad. Rafael ordered the filet stuffed with lobster and crab with a white wine sauce, steamed vegetables, pasta, and salad.

"Are we hungry tonight?" I asked teasingly.

"I am going to need all the energy I can get."

He smiled back at me and leaned closer to me to kiss me and he reached for my hand. He led it under his coat and to the crotch of his pants. He wanted me to feel him, like he needed to feel my touch. I felt the same way. I rubbed my hand along the length of his erection and tickled it with the tips of my fingers through his pants. He started whispering in my ear in Spanish as I led his hands between the slit in my gown. He felt the lace panties and moaned in my ear. His breathing was getting faster, as was mine. With all the people around us, it added to the excitement and arousal. I started kissing his ear and played with it with my tongue, sucking it into my mouth, and then moved to his neck when I felt him slow down and his muscles tighten. I pulled back to see his face and the look was terrifying.

"I hate not being able to hear what you can, what's going on?" Rafael was silent for several minutes before he spoke.

"Mr. Sanchez is my uncle," He said in total disbelief, and then continued, "I never knew my father; my mother left Spain when I was born, and we ended up in Miami. It's all coming together now. This is why my mother left Spain. My mother never spoke of my father. Now I know it was to protect me from the life she left. I never asked about my father. I never wanted to know either. I always thought if he was a good man, he would have been with us." Rafael looked confused. I just looked at him and waited to see what he was going to do or say. He was very quiet. Our salads came and he ate silently, giving me a smile and wink every once in a while. It was his way of letting me know he was still here, but he really wasn't. His mind was going a mile a minute, and he was talking back to the people communicating with him. I just watched. He was just as entertaining as I had been to him in the last few days. Watching his facial movements, his hand movements, and where his eyes looked, I was imagining my own scenarios, hearing only half of the conversation.

I started looking around the room again. I watched all the beautiful people enjoying the evening, but I was waiting for something to go terribly wrong. I saw Mr. Sanchez and he looked at me just then. I smiled, and excused myself from Rafael and his conversation with his salad.

"Where are you going?" Rafael looked up to me.

"To the ladies room." I raised one eyebrow, not in a sneaky way, just to say I needed to go to the bathroom.

"I'm coming with you."

"I think I can manage."

"Let's go find the ladies room then," Rafael replied with a cocked eyebrow like he was up to something.

"Fine, but you can wait outside." I turned around and started walking into one of the hallways, Rafael following right behind me. I saw one door open and it was a very large and luxurious bathroom. I turned around and kissed Rafael, then entered the room, closing the door behind me.

I laughed to myself as I stood inside the door of the ornate bathroom with its seating area and separate room for the toilet. I laid my purse on the counter and went to the bathroom. I returned to the marble counter with the built-in sink, turned the gold faucets, and washed my hands. Rafael must have heard the water because he came in and locked the door behind him. I dried my hands and used some of the moisturizer that was also on the counter. Rafael came up behind me and kissed my neck. I watched him in the mirror. The tenderness was showing on his face and in the way he kissed me. He looked at me in the mirror watching him, then bent down and touched my ankles. The palms of his hands moved up the sides of my legs to my thighs, lifting parts of my gown with them until he was standing behind me touching my hips and feeling my panties. We watched each other in the mirror. I loved how sensual it felt. I wanted to touch him, but I knew he was already torturing himself right now. I wasn't sure how much his jacket could hide if I did. I slowly turned around, and he let go of my gown and it fell back to the floor. I touched his face and stared at him for just a second, and then my eyes went to his lips. They were so full and soft. I touched my lips against his; he joined in softly, kissing me back. We gently took turns kissing each other's lips. I put my hands inside his jacket to feel his chest. I felt his shoulder holster, and something underneath his shirt.

"Are you wearing bullet proof clothes?" I asked Rafael.

"You are too."

I turned around and looked in the mirror. No wonder the bodice and left sleeve of this gown was so heavy. Wow they had come a long way in bullet proof gear. I looked at Rafael in the mirror and smiled.

"What are you smiling about?" Rafael asked me.

"I feel like a superhero, my son would love this." Hayden and I were always playing some villain vs. good guy game that Hayden would make up as we went along. I just needed my light saber. I shook my head and laughed.

"Are you done here?" He looked serious.

"Yes, but first tell me what is happening. You're so easy to read." I smirked at him.

"People are starting to leave; it could be a good distraction. We should get back to the ballroom." He reached for my hand and started to walk to the door.

"Wait. I need to fix my make-up." I let go of his hand and reached for my purse. I applied more lipstick and gloss then turned to Rafael and said,

"Okay now I'm ready." I started to laugh and he did too, shaking his head like he didn't understand at all. That's okay, most men don't.

I took his hand and we left the bathroom and walked down the hallway and out to the main room. He kept me behind him walking through the people and to our table. He set my purse down and asked if I would dance with him. I nodded and he led me to the open floor. Even though I did notice people were saying goodbye, there were still many people here. Rafael held me close to him. We were both just looking at the people around the room, yet it was hard to concentrate feeling his body so close to mine. We danced for about fifteen minutes, maybe longer. I had no concept of time. He looked at me and asked if I wanted to take some wine outside. I nodded again. We went to our table to retrieve my purse, and he motioned to someone to get a bottle of the wine we were drinking and send it outside on the veranda. This time he walked behind me as we made our way outside.

I went to another seating area with sofas and chairs circling the fireplace. It was hot inside dancing, but it was cooling down outside, and the warmth from the fire felt lovely on my skin. We sat close together on the sofa. The outdoor furniture was beautiful wrought iron. The cushions and pillows were all in shades of reds and tans. Smoke from cigarettes and cigars combined with the scents of vanilla candles lingered in the air. The waiter came over with our red wine and left the bottle. He whispered to Rafael that everything was taken care of. I assumed the waiter was in on the mission, but I had never seen him before. Rafael nodded and asked him to find some more cigarettes. He obviously planned on sitting out here for a while.

"I thought we should be inside," I commented.

"It's safer for you out here. There is nothing we intend to take into our own hands right now, and I'd rather be out of the line of fire."

We sat drinking our wine, listening to the music and watching the people who were outside on the veranda.

"What are you smiling about?" I asked him.

"You golf, too." He looked impressed.

"I used to. My girlfriends and I kept a standing tee time every Monday morning for years, hitting the clubhouse after the ninth hole and then again after we finished the back nine. We smoked cigars and played competitively just against each other with some friendly monetary bets, but that seems like a lifetime ago. Do you golf?"

"No, I don't. You like cigars?" He was shaking his head again.

"I like to live in the moment. I wish it didn't take losing my mother to learn to live my life, but sometimes it takes something like that for you to appreciate life itself," I said in a reminiscent tone.

He leaned in to kiss me and I met him there. If it weren't for the crowd, I would have taken him right there on the couch. I pulled away and asked him,

"Is there something you want to talk about, Mr. Montoya?"

I looked into those gorgeous eyes and could see through to his soul, like he just let me in.

He leaned to whisper in my ear about making love to me, speaking in his native tongue. He started kissing my neck and shoulder when I said,

"I was talking about something else, maybe your father?"

He never stopped kissing me, but when he got to my ear again he whispered,

"No."

He pulled away to sip his wine, and grabbed the pack of cigarettes that seemed to magically appear on the table. He lit one and handed it to me, then lit one for himself and looked at me. I just waited. The wine was wonderful; I looked at the bottle to see what it was. There were only a few Spanish red wines I liked, but this one I would try to remember. I looked back to Rafael, still waiting for him to say something. He just looked relaxed and content. Maybe he wasn't going to say anything at all. We sat back against the couch and enjoyed the view. Every star was out tonight and the moon was especially bright and glorious.

Luis stepped in front of our view and asked if he could join us.

"Of course, please do," I said. Rafael was silent. Luis pulled up one of the chairs closer to the sofa where we were sitting. He pulled out a cigar and lit it. He made eye contact with Rafael and then looked at me.

"I'm sorry I deceived you Mrs. Montoya; the letter I gave you was for Rafael, from his father. I promised that I would give it to him someday. I wasn't sure if Rafael knew who I was or if he would find out tonight, but I needed to give him that letter even if it was the last thing I did." Luis looked steadily at Rafael. My eyes traveled back and forth between them, waiting for someone to say something. Rafael was staring at the ground and my eyes met Luis'. I didn't know what to say to break the silence. I touched Rafael's face and turned his head to look at me. That soul I saw earlier was gone. He looked empty.

"Thank you Luis, could you please give us a moment. We'll see you again inside, if you don't mind." I smiled at him like he was someone I knew and cared for. He nodded his head and walked away. I looked back to Rafael and put both my hands against his face. I just stared into his lifeless eyes and wondered about the source of the pain.

"Would you like to dance with me?" I asked him. I could be close to him, hold him and love him at the same time. He didn't answer, so I just pulled his hand when I stood and took him to the dance floor. I left everything there. I saw the waiter from earlier and motioned to our belongings on the table. He knew exactly what I was asking. My purse was in good hands, and the letter that was inside it.

I noticed when we went inside that more people had left and it was down to about half now. Still about fifty people, if I had to guess. We made it to the center of the dance floor and he grabbed my waist. He pulled me into him with one hand holding mine and the other on my ass. I was at least four inches taller in my stilettos which put me closer to his face. I kissed underneath his chin, and then he dipped me down and kissed me in the same place. He pulled me up and we were face to face, moving to the music. I could feel him against me, his heat on my skin, and his lips against mine. I couldn't have felt closer to him at that moment. I looked into his eyes searching for that soul and feeling I saw earlier, but it still wasn't there. There was just pain. I wanted to take it away from him.

"Please talk to me about what you are feeling." I stared at him, pleading for him to let me in.

"I'm not really sure what I'm feeling to be honest. I don't know if I want to know about my father. What would he have to say to me? I never knew him."

He moved around the dance floor, one of my legs between his as he pulled me closer. He didn't want to talk about it right now, that much I got. I didn't want to push him, so I left it alone. I enjoyed his body moving mine. It was cosmic the way we moved together. I was really enjoying dancing, but was starting to get tired.

"How much longer do we have to stay?" I whispered in his ear.

"I've been waiting for you to ask me that all night. Are you ready to leave?"

I nodded and he stopped dancing and kissed me. The world seemed to be standing still again. I didn't even hear the music anymore.

Chapter 21

From behind Rafael, I heard a shot, looked in the direction it came, and then quickly to where it went. I was startled by the loud noise and suddenly realized we were directly between the shooter and Mr. Sanchez. Then another shot from the other side of the room. I turned Rafael in the opposite direction and tried to push him to the side as he grabbed my hand. Within seconds more shots were fired and the first shooter was down. I was still pushing Rafael in front of me to get out of the way when Rafael grabbed me around the waist. I heard one more shot and saw Luis fall to the ground. I started to feel the most intense pain and burning in my shoulder.

Everyone was running and dropping to the floor for cover as Rafael and I were still trying to get out of the way. I saw Kit and Rock ducking behind a table keeping their eyes on the situation. I imagined that they were all talking together and communicating about the shooters, and then everything went quiet and the shooting stopped. People were in a panic, screaming, crying and trying to get out of the mansion.

I could hear horns outside and I could see a lot of blood around the room. I started to wonder if I were going to pass out, not from the blood, but from the absolute unreal situation that was happening. I looked back to Luis on the floor, blood pooling around him. He knew this was going to happen, yet it didn't make it easier for me to deal with. Rafael grabbed me around the shoulders and pulled me next to him. I was shaking, but I wasn't cold. We made it to the entrance and walked out to the car in front of the circle. Rafael took off his coat and put it around my shoulders. I started to get in the car and remembered my purse. Rafael asked Kit to grab it on the veranda outside and bring it to the villa when everything was taken care of. Then he got in the car too. We pulled away in a hurry like everyone else. As we made it out of the gate, I saw the police cars and ambulances pulling up to the gate. Rafael put his arm around me, and when he touched my shoulder I winced. Rafael didn't notice. He was just watching everything taking place. My shoulder was really burning, and I didn't know why. I sat back in the seat and closed my eyes, trying to reach my new happy place.

We made it back to the villa and went inside. The driver went back to get the others. Rafael walked into the kitchen and poured a drink. I went to the bedroom and into the bathroom. I took off Rafael's jacket and hung it on one of the towel hooks. I noticed that it looked wet on the shoulder and down one arm. I turned around to look in the mirror and saw all the blood running down my arm. I started to panic, and then I grabbed a towel and held it there. Rafael walked into the bathroom and saw the blood running down my arm and he froze for just a second. He put down his drink and one he had brought for me on the counter and removed the towel from my shoulder.

"Maya, what happened?" His look was horrifying.

"I don't really know. I just heard a shot and then felt this burning feeling. Everything happened so fast." He went for a first aid kit and started to clean my arm so that we could see where all the blood was coming from. It hurt like hell now, and I reached for one of the drinks. I took a sip first to see what it was. Whiskey. I drank the entire glass and put the glass down.

"Maya, we have to get you to a hospital." He looked at me and then was talking to the driver that dropped us off, trying to determine his location.

"No, I hate hospitals. Just kiss it and give me a sucker." I smiled wanly. It worked for my four-year-old. Whenever he got hurt, he just asked me to kiss it with my magic kisses and then he wanted a sucker. All is healed.

"Damn it, Maya, I can't get it to stop bleeding." He threw down the towel and reached for another.

"Rafael." I waited for him to look at me, "Calm down. Does anyone on your team know some basic sewing?"

He started talking to his contacts and ordered Kit and Rock to get the rest of the team out and get to the villa, asking them to bring any medical supplies they could find. Then he said something about fifteen minutes. I reached with my other arm for the glasses on the counter and took the full one. I handed it to Rafael, and he drank it in one mouthful.

"Would you like another?" he asked me and I happily nodded just to give him something else to do. I went to the small loveseat in the bathroom and took off my dress. It was totally ruined, not even salvageable. I hung it back on the hanger, grabbed a fresh towel, and held it against my shoulder as I sat on the loveseat and kicked off my shoes. I put my feet up and Rafael walked into the bathroom.

"You know my team will be here soon. Maybe we should put some clothes on you." He stopped at the door and looked at me.

"And I thought the panties were too much." I laughed trying to take his mind off the blood pouring from my shoulder. He walked toward me, handed me a glass, and we toasted to not getting killed tonight. We both drank the whiskey in one shot, and Rafael went for my robe that was laying across the end of the bed. I put my good arm through the sleeve and Rafael covered me with the other half. I rested my head against the back of the cushions and looked at Rafael.

"Kiss me," I said to him.

He bent down next to the loveseat and leaned against my leg. I closed my eyes and felt his lips on mine, passionate kisses, like he needed to make up for something. Maybe it was a combination of the excitement, the agony of seeing me hurt, and the build-up of a day's worth of foreplay that hit him suddenly. He was breathing heavily, and I felt his heart race. He felt strong against me as he held pressure to the towel on my shoulder. He pulled his body close to mine until there was no space between us. He moved between my legs and revealed part of my stomach and panties. He groaned like he couldn't wait any longer, then we heard Kit yell, "Maya! Rafael!" as she burst through the front door of the villa. He laid his head against my stomach and tried to catch his breath.

"We're in the bathroom," Rafael called back.

Kit came around the corner then Rock and then Tex and Techno were standing in the doorway from the bedroom to the bathroom.

"Come on in, the more the merrier," I said with as much energy as I could muster. I was feeling the last two shots of whiskey and the pain wasn't as bad as it was just minutes earlier. Kit was already checking out my shoulder and Rock was getting out medical supplies. Rafael stepped back and looked at me with great concern; I winked at him and turned my head to look at my shoulder.

"Kit, is my eye make-up still good?" I asked playfully. I wanted to see her face after looking at my shoulder.

"Gorgeous." She looked at me like nothing was wrong, and I knew everything was going to be fine.

"That's what I call my son." I said to her and thought of Hayden. He was just the sweetest little boy ever. He would always tell me I was so beautiful, and I would tell him that he was gorgeous in return. He had always been an equal amount of both Matt and I, but he got all the good from the two of us. I loved him so much. He would be freaking out right now from the blood. He didn't like anything that showed blood.

Rafael stood there with a stunned look on his face. I was sure that he was having a hard time seeing me like this.

"Mr. Montoya, would you like to order us all some food since we didn't get to eat dinner or have dessert yet?"

"Yes, that sounds good." He turned around and walked out of the room. He had a smirk on his face at least. I nodded to Techno. He was the one always keeping them in communication with each other. The man behind all the high tech gizmos, I assumed.

"Will you please go keep Rafael company and amused for a while? He's not doing so well right now."

He nodded and I looked back to my shoulder just in time to see a huge needle about to go into my arm.

"What the hell is that?" My eyes went wide at the sight of the needle. I didn't want anything to put me out.

"It's just going to help with the pain," Rock said.

"It won't knock me out, right? I do have plans for tonight." I gave him my dead serious look. Rock gave me the shot anyway.

They cleaned up my shoulder, and I was thrilled to hear there was no bullet lodged in my body. It only grazed the outside of my shoulder. It was going to take many stitches to put the gash back together again, but it could have been a lot worse.

"I'm going to pour this on the wound and it's going to hurt, a lot," Rock said, and Kit gave me a warning look and grabbed for my hand.

"Thanks for the heads up!" I started with nervous laughter in anticipation of the hurt. I laugh whenever I feel pain; I can't explain it. While getting my first tattoo, I was laughing so hard that the artist made a couple of mistakes from my jerking around like I was being tickled. Even with this quirk, I was much better with physical pain than emotional pain any day. I could handle this. I could feel the cold liquid as Rock poured the alcohol on my wound.

"Oh, yeah, that would be the pain." I closed my eyes and smiled but tried not to laugh. I went to my happy place again. I stayed silent with my eyes shut for a while and I heard Kit say,

"Good as new." I opened my eyes and looked at Kit and Rock.

"That's all?" Wow I wondered if I had passed out at all during that time, or if my happy place really kept my mind busy that long. Then I looked at Rock, Kit and Tex standing there.

"Are we all ready for a cigarette and a drink or what?" I laughed really hard, like it just hit me all at once.

Rock kissed me on the forehead and said I had them all worried to death.

"That was Rafael's doing, not mine. He's been freaking out since we got back. Thank you for fixing me up." I kissed him on the cheek and he stood up and walked out with Tex following behind him. Kit stayed with me and helped me up just as Rafael walked into the bathroom.

"How are you?"

"I'm fine, but starving and dying to have a cigarette, so let's go outside and enjoy the rest of the evening." Then I remembered.

"Oh, Kit, did you get my purse?" I turned around to look at her.

"It's in the kitchen."

They all heard the conversations tonight and the matter of Rafael's father. There was also the letter still in my purse. I wanted to make sure it was still there. Kit pulled the other side of the robe over my shoulder and tied the belt. I kissed her on the cheek and hugged her with the one arm I could feel.

"Thank you," I said pulling away. Rafael took my arm and led me out to the patio. By the looks of the towels and rags in the garbage, I had lost a lot of blood. I felt okay considering what I had just been through. I was really happy that this mission was mostly over, or so I hoped. Rafael still had some things to deal with as far as his part in this mission and also learning about his uncle and father, but he would deal with that when he was ready.

We all sat around the large table and Rock came out with a bottle of something under his arm, didn't matter what at this point, and glasses in each hand. He started pouring and passing the drinks around the table until everyone had one. Strangely, everyone became silent. They all seemed to be quietly in their own thoughts. I looked at each of them and then to Rafael. He was looking at me so seriously. I raised my brow, wondering what he was thinking about. His eyes looked lighter in color with a slight twinkle in them. I looked up to see where the moon was, knowing it was always close by. It was the most spectacular moon I had ever seen, so big and brilliant. I looked back at Rafael and he was still staring at me intently.

"To fat ladies that sing," Rock said and held up his glass. I started laughing so hard. I knew the saying that something isn't over until the fat lady sings. Then I realized it was an inside joke, and my laughing started to make everyone else laugh too. We all toasted and touched our glasses together and downed the whiskey. Someone passed around a pack of cigarettes and everyone took one. I suddenly realized I was having a hard time with my left arm, like I couldn't feel it. Good thing I was right handed.

I refocused on the people sitting around me and noticed that all of them were talking to one another. They spoke in English, but for some reason I felt like I didn't understand any of the conversations going on at all. Rafael whispered in my ear,

"Are you okay?" He touched my face. I didn't even see him come around to me.

I turned my head to the sound of his voice,

"I'm fine." It was a lie. I was not feeling fine at all. I was hoping that the food would come soon. I felt like I was hallucinating and lightheaded. I couldn't focus and my head was pounding. I felt his lips touch mine, and I used it as an excuse to close my eyes for a second.

I heard a knock and Kit went inside to open the door. Rock followed behind her. It was our dinner and I was glad to see it. Rafael joined Kit and Rock and brought plates and silverware out to the table along with all the food. I sat back in my chair and rested my head against the back. I closed my eyes and just relaxed for a few minutes. I felt bad that I wasn't helping, but I didn't think I could stand up right now, much less be of any help. The world starting spinning and I felt everything go quiet and dark.

22
Chapter

I opened my eyes and noticed I was in bed propped up on a mountain of pillows, and I heard music. I listened for a few minutes and it was angelic. It sounded like someone was playing the piano in the villa. I took my time standing up, still feeling a little off, and walked slowly out to the living room. I didn't see anyone. I looked out to the deck, toward the kitchen and dining room, and started walking toward the front of the villa. I hadn't been in any of the front rooms since we'd been here. I was drawn to the passion of the music, and I reached a room off the front hallway. I walked in and discovered a sitting room with a fireplace and a grand piano. I stood there watching Rafael sitting at the piano. He had his back to me so he couldn't see that I was there. He was only wearing the pants to his tux, no shirt. I walked behind him and straddled the piano bench next to him and put one of my legs over his. He continued to play until the song was over. I saw the letter from his father on the piano. He had read it. I could tell by the anguish in his face. He finally turned his head to look at me.

"Are you okay?" I asked him, worried about what was in the letter and how he was feeling about what he read. I pulled a piece of his hair out of his face and put it behind his ear and ran my fingers along the side of his face.

"I haven't been very good at protecting you, I've been so worried about you. We had to give you blood earlier. You could have died. And you're asking me if I'm okay?" He looked at me like he was about to fall apart, and his eyes filled with tears. I reached across his back to pull him closer to me. I kissed him and I felt the tears leave his eyes and reach our lips. I tried to pull away, but he pulled me closer. His mouth grew more intense, stronger and more passionate. He touched my face with both his hands and finally, slowly pulled away. It was there, his soul, searching mine, that look in his eyes that invited me deep inside him. His eyes were magical, mysterious and wanting.

"Did you read the letter?" I asked him sweetly.

"Yes. It doesn't change anything. I never knew him and will never know him." He looked at me.

"So you play the piano? Any other skills I need to know about?" He moved to the side of my face and I felt his breath on my ear. He whispered,

"I have many special skills but I'd rather show you than tell you." He found my lips again with all his emotion. I wrapped my other leg around the back of him and he completely lifted me off the bench and onto his lap with my behind almost touching the keys. He reached both hands inside my robe and opened the top of it to show my breasts. His fingers touched me so softly, like he was afraid of hurting me. It was still painful to try and move my left arm. I put my hands on his chest and he laid his head against mine. His ear was close to my heart, which was beating a little faster than normal. I reached my arm around him, caressed his hair, and held his head close me, comforting him. He seemed so relaxed right now I didn't want to ruin it by saying anything.

Suddenly he picked me up and carried me into the kitchen and sat me on the counter.

"You need to eat something," he said as he opened the refrigerator and took out a plate of food. He put it in the microwave for a few minutes and poured me a glass of water from a pitcher with ice and slices of lemon. I sat there watching him. He was as animated as I was when he was thinking. He took out the plate and walked in front of me, pushing my legs apart to get close enough to feed me.

"What is it?" I asked.

"Grilled salmon with a lemon butter sauce." He brought a fork full up to my mouth and finally made eye contact with me. I took it in my mouth and it melted.

"It's delicious. You remembered my favorite dish. Thank you." I took another bite and chewed slowly. "You know I'm not handicapped. I can feed myself."

"I know." He laughed.

"Did everyone else get to eat this time?"

"Eventually. You passed out when the food came, and we had to call in a doctor. He gave you two units of blood, fluids, and antibiotics so you don't get an infection. You've been out for about four hours, and I still can't believe you are up and walking around. You should still be in bed."

"Oh, I plan on spending whatever time we have left together in bed. I think I'll be fine." I giggled at him and took another bite. He grinned at me and took his phone out of his pocket. He pushed one button, then I took it away from him and waited until someone answered while we playfully glared at each other.

"Hey, how is she?" Rock said before I could get a hello in.

"I'm doing great; did you have the salmon tonight? It's amazing; it just melts in your mouth." I took another bite and waited for him to say something.

"Maya, what are you doing up. You should be out like a light. How are you feeling? We've all been worried sick." He really sounded upset. For one big ass guy, and they don't call him Rock for nothing, he sure could be mushy.

"Well, I'm up and I'm doing fine, really. Thank you all for helping me."

"Anytime and anywhere. If you ever need us, we'll be there. I mean that Maya," Rock said softly.

"Thanks again. Here's Rafael. Please tell the team that I'm fine." I handed the phone to Rafael and he smirked at me.

As Rafael walked into the living room, I got down from the counter and went to use the bathroom. I closed the door behind me and could still hear Rafael talking. I really felt fine, just sore. I managed to take the pins out of my hair and brush it a little. I brushed my teeth and washed my hands. I was putting lotion on when I heard a knock at the door.

"Are you doing okay?" he asked.

"I'm great. I'll be out in a minute." I looked at my face and thanked God for waterproof make-up. My eyes still looked perfect. I added the usual gloss on my lips, and even with that, they weren't as soft as Rafael's were.

I walked out to the living room and sat next to Rafael on the couch. I leaned my head against him.

"How's your shoulder?" he asked.

I looked up at him, and he looked a little more relieved that I seemed to be doing okay.

"I'm fine," I said as he raised his eyebrows at me.

"I've been shot before, and it hurts like hell. How can you be fine?" He shook his head.

"I'm fine because you are here, and I don't feel alone for the first time in my life. My shoulder will heal. When you touch me, kiss me, look at me, and make love to me, it makes me want more out of my life. When I look into your eyes, I can see your soul. You are so beautiful, and I don't know how I'm going to let you go. You've given me so much, and I want to give you the same things." I stared at him trying to hold back the tears. "I believe you can love anyone you let into your heart, because I love you. I wish I could give you more, but I can't."

He kissed me like he shared the pain. He held my face like he was never going to let go. When he finally pulled away, he looked at me with the eyes from the first night, tormented and sad. I wondered if it showed in my eyes as well.

"Do you want to go outside and sit?" he asked me.

"That sounds nice."

We both stood, and he started to pick me up.

"Rafael, I can walk."

"Maya, for once can you stop being so stubborn, and just let me love you and take care of you." He picked me up and carried me to the table and chairs outside on the deck. "Do you want to finish your dinner?" he asked as I sat down.

"No, but I'd love a glass of wine."

He walked back inside, brought out a bottle and two glasses, sat next to me, and poured our wine. As usual, he lit a cigarette and handed it to me, and then lit one for himself. I wondered what time it was. The sun had to be coming up soon. I sipped my wine and looked at Rafael. He was looking at the moon, quiet in his own thoughts. I watched him. He rested his head on the back of the chair. His face showed no emotion.

"What are you thinking about?" I asked him.

"The letter." He put his cigarette out and I did the same.

"Do you want to talk about it?" I said, and he finally turned his head to look at me.

"No." He barely shook his head.

"Rafael, what did the waiter at the party mean when he said that everything was taken care of?" I looked at him wondering.

"Dessert." he said and his face lit up.

I hadn't seen that smile since we left the party. He stood up and picked me up from the chair, he carried me in silence down the stairs to the gardens, and then down to the shore. I didn't say or ask anything. I was just curious. As we got to the sand, he turned to the side and I saw it. There was the most elegant bed I had ever seen sitting high on the beach next to the rock ledge, all white and glowing against the light of the moon. It stood out like it was the only thing that existed. He looked at me, and he started walking toward the bed.

The ocean was quiet, the waves slow and calm. The breeze was light but cool. It was all so magnificent. He let my legs fall to the sand, and I stood still holding on to him. He untied my robe and dropped it to the sand. He picked me up again and laid me on the bed, so gently. My shoulder was bandaged, and I could see blood coming through. I was just hoping it wouldn't ruin the moment. He lay on the bed next to me and touched his hand to my neck, feeling my skin, touching my breasts and then resting his hand against the beat of my heart. He was just staring at me. I wondered if he could see into my soul as well.

"Do you think we were meant to cross each other's path?"

"Yes." I answered, and he dropped his head to hide the rush of tears. "It's not until you are lost, that you can be found," I said and touched his face. I moved my hand down to his chest and rested it against the beat of his heart. He leaned down to kiss me. The moon was watching us, like it had several times this week. I closed my eyes and felt his mouth move from my lips, down my chin and neck to my breasts. He kissed me from head to toe, feeling my skin with his lips and tongue. I wanted him so badly. I wanted to love him as much as I could, for as long as I had left. He returned his mouth to mine and whispered close to my lips,

"I love you."

It took my breath away. That whole week had just been so incredible and surreal.

"Show me Rafael, show me how much you love me," I whispered back to him. I took his mouth with mine and we kissed like it was our last kiss, never wanting it to end. I felt his body against mine, his heart beating as fast as mine. My body was enveloped by his, and I felt the heat from his body warming mine. I reached down to undo his pants button. He reached for my hand and put it above my head and held it there. His mouth left my lips, and I watched him, holding me so close to him, moving his mouth down my neck to my breasts. He played with my nipples with his tongue licking me down to my navel. He had to let go of my hand to move lower, but I left it there. He pleasured me over and over before finally undoing his pants, removing them, and then his briefs. I thought I would die if I didn't feel him inside me soon. He lay on top of me and kissed me so slowly before I felt him between my legs. He made love to me by the light of the moon until dawn came upon us. We fell asleep in each other's arms as the sun started to rise.

23
Chapter

I woke up feeling parched. The sun was bright above us and Rafael was snoring softly. I felt lightheaded and wasn't sure whether it was exhaustion or dehydration. Probably both.

I watched Rafael sleep, his face so soft and sweet. He was almost smiling. I touched his cheek with my fingers and outlined his lips with my fingertips. I needed to go to the bathroom, but I didn't want to leave him here and have him wake up alone. I tickled the outside of his mouth, and he swatted my hand away and opened his eyes. I was smiling at him when he looked at me.

"Good morning, Mr. Montoya, I hope you slept well." I said and kissed him on his chin and nose and then his lips. He smiled a huge smile and said,

"Good morning to you Mrs. Montoya." He kissed me and then finished, "I slept a little too well. What time is it?"

I laughed at him.

"You're asking me? I don't bother with the time." I smirked at him.

"The doctor and my team were going to be at the villa first thing this morning to check on you." He kissed me again.

"Well, I can tell you we missed first thing this morning hours ago." I kissed his ear and whispered, "Maybe we should get back." Not that I wanted to move from that spot, but I did need something to drink.

"Yes, I guess we should." He looked at me sadly. He stood up and had the usual morning erection. When I saw him like that standing in front of me, I forgot everything else and pulled him back on top of me. I rolled him on his back and sat up on him. I couldn't move my left arm, the pain was so intense. I grabbed the headboard with my right hand and lifted myself up enough to place his erection inside me. I stared at him while I took him, all of him, and moaned in sweet pleasure. He closed his eyes, but I still watched him as I made love to him. I touched his chest and his muscles down to his abdomen. I could feel his heart beating against my hand. I leaned down to kiss him, and at that angle I could feel us both getting close. I wanted to watch the pleasure in his face and eyes. We came together as I kissed his neck, and I could feel his breathing against my skin. I sucked on his ear as we relaxed, and I whispered how he made me feel.

He wrapped the sheet around us both and picked me up from the bed with him still inside me. He carried me, holding me so tightly, back to the villa as I rested my head on his shoulder. He took me into the bathroom and closed the door. He kissed me again with all his emotion and said he'd be right back. He went to the closet and pulled out a pair of cargo shorts and a T-shirt, put them on and walked out of the bedroom, closing the door behind him. I heard him talking to everyone in the living room and kitchen.

I washed my face and brushed my teeth, happy to see the color returning to my face. I went to the closet to find something to wear when Rafael came back into the bedroom.

"Can you please help me get dressed?" I asked feeling helpless.

"It would be my pleasure, but if it were up to me, I'd keep you naked." He looked sad even though he tried to smile.

"What's wrong?"

"Our department chief is on his way here to discuss our next job and debrief the event from last night." He kissed me as he helped me get dressed.

"Is that a bad thing?" I asked.

"No, I'm just afraid that we may have to leave earlier than I want to."

We finished getting my clothes on, he kissed me again, afraid our time might be cut short, and lingered, holding me tightly against him.

"The doctor is waiting to check on you. We should go." He held my hand and we walked into the living room together.

The whole team and the doctor were in the main living area, talking and eating. When they saw us come out of the bedroom, they all stopped to look at us. The doctor walked toward me and introduced himself. He was amazed at how well I was doing. He had me sit down and starting taking my vitals.

"Good morning," I said finally getting a moment in between everyone asking me how I was doing, and happy to see that I was fine.

"Maya, you're like superwoman without the kryptonite. Is there anything that can break you?" Rock asked and they all laughed.

"What, you didn't know I was trained to be a superhero?" I quickly retorted.

The doctor removed my bandages and looked at the wound.

"I'm just going to clean it up a little, give you something for the pain, and then some fluids with an antibiotic. I'm surprised you're doing so well. I wanted to take you to the hospital last night, but Rafael wouldn't let us."

I looked at Rafael and mouthed, "Thank you." He knew I wouldn't want to go if I had the choice, and he stood his ground because I obviously couldn't. I was grateful he respected my wishes.

Rafael brought me a glass of water and some toast. I was never so happy to see water and toast before. He sat next to me on the couch and fed me bites. I felt so pitiful, which wasn't a feeling I was used to.

"You seem like you're doing okay. I was worried last night, but I can see you're stronger than I thought. You need to take it easy for a few days and follow up with a doctor when you get home." The doctor looked at me and smiled like he knew something I didn't.

"I'm done here, so take care of yourself. It was nice meeting you."

"Thank you for everything," I said and he said goodbye to everyone and walked toward the door. Rafael followed behind him, showing him out and talking with him before I heard the door open and close.

Rafael walked back into the room and stood in the kitchen. Everyone was very quiet, and I was starting to wonder what was going on. I just sat there leaning back on the couch and put my feet on the coffee table.

"Okay, is someone going to tell me what's going on, or are we just going to stare at each other all day?" I said jokingly.

Techno stood up and walked toward me. He sat on the couch next to me and explained how he had been monitoring my phone and that my husband had called.

"That's it? That's why you all are acting like the end of the world is coming?" Then I wondered if something was wrong at home. "Techno, can you get me a phone that will show up on my caller ID at home with my number on it?" I asked suddenly in a panic, hoping everything at home was alright.

"Give me two minutes." He stood up and went to his laptop.

I walked outside to have a cigarette and sit down to wait for a phone. No one followed me, and the silence in the villa was starting to make me very uneasy. Techno came out to the deck and handed me a phone.

"Thank you," I said and he walked back inside.

I dialed my home number and waited for Matt to answer.

"Hello, I've been trying to reach you," he said rudely.

"You know that I don't get a signal here, and the whole building is having trouble with their phone lines. So hi, how are you?" I said in my usual sarcastic way.

"I'm fine. We just wanted to know when you were coming home." He sounded annoyed.

"I'll be home in time to decorate for Halloween. I don't know how long my phone is going to hold out. Can I talk to Hayden?" I heard him sigh and give the phone to my son.

"Hi Mommy!" He sounded so excited.

"Hi, gorgeous, how was your camping trip?" I asked and smiled, as the tears started to well up in my eyes.

"It was scary, mom. There were a lot of bugs and monsters at night! We made marshmallows on the fire and we went fishing, but I didn't catch anything. We used worms, they were gross!"

"Well, I miss you baby, and I'll be home soon so we can get ready for Halloween and carve our pumpkin. Did you pick a pattern for it yet?" The tears were running down my face by now, and it was hard not to let him hear the sadness in my voice.

"No, Daddy said we would find one today. I miss you mommy. Daddy doesn't do things like you."

"Well, you be a good boy, and I'll be home before you know it. I love you, gorgeous."

"I love you more, mommy. Come home soon." He blew me a kiss on the phone and I blew one back.

"Okay angel, let me talk to daddy before my phone dies. Find a good face for our pumpkin." I could barely talk I was crying so hard. He handed the phone to Matt,

"Hi," he said.

"Why do you sound so angry?" I asked.

"I just hadn't heard from you and didn't know when you planned on coming home," he said rudely again.

"I didn't know I had a curfew. I'll be home early Sunday," I said just as snotty as he sounded. This was our problem, and here I thought the time away would make us miss each other and appreciate each other. "What's really going on, Matt?"

"I guess I'll see you Sunday then," and he hung up the phone.

I knew what the problem was; Matt didn't know how to be a father. Since Hayden was born, everything he did seemed more important than his family. He was never home and all the responsibility fell on me. He acted like he worked and went to school and that was all he should be expected to do. Provide. That wasn't at all what I had in mind, not what I thought a family should be. I thought I would have a partner in life and a man that loved me and our son. I knew he loved us, but as far as being partners and a family, it just hadn't worked out that way so far.

That last week, the implications of the affair had crept into my head, and I started feeling guilty. I could rationalize it the way I usually do, but the truth was I had betrayed him as well. I hadn't done it on purpose. It just happened and although it filled an emptiness I had inside temporarily, it wouldn't change the problems in my life.

When I leave here, I thought, I will be just as alone as when I came.

Rafael walked out to me and sat at the table.

"Is everything okay?" He looked at me with no expression.

"Just another day in paradise!" I laughed and started crying at the same time.

He leaned over to me, grabbing me and holding me so tightly. I sobbed in his arms, and the rest of the team came out and joined in holding me. All of a sudden I started to laugh. It seemed almost funny to me that these people I had only known for a week were so kind and understanding, more than my husband had been in years. And he was the man I swore to love and cherish for the rest of my life!

"Okay, I think it's time to have a little fun before the boss man comes. Who's in?" I asked and smiled at all their sympathetic faces. "We're going to need a bottle of whiskey, some cigars and a deck of cards," I said trying to seem lighthearted.

Everyone laughed and started to stand up, then Rock stopped and looked at Rafael. I looked at him and asked,

"What is it?"

"I just got a call that Mrs. Sanchez came home this morning to plan the funeral arrangements." Rafael looked down. "I want to go talk to her," he said and looked back to me.

"Do you want me to go with you?" I asked worried about him.

"No, I think this is something I need to do on my own." I was proud of him. He needed to do this. I knew that he probably had many questions he needed answers to. After all, he just found out that he had an aunt and two cousins, and watched his uncle die in front of him last night.

I nodded to him and smiled. He kissed me and I could feel him trembling.

"It's going to be okay," I said and he walked away telling his team to take good care of me and to remember the boss man would be here in about seven hours, "Don't be drunken fools when he arrives," said Rafael. We all made a serious face and everyone went inside the villa with Rafael, except Tex. He was the most polite man, shy almost. I don't usually assume things about people. If I did, I'd say with that accent and belt buckle, he grew up on a horse farm in Texas. I could have been wrong, but I doubted it. He pulled up the chair next to mine and sat down. He reached his hand to cover my hands in my lap.

"What is it Tex?"

"Maya, I wish I could slap some sense into your husband, but I wouldn't unless you asked me." He smiled like he really wanted to.

"What do you mean?" I had no idea where this was going.

"I was married before and had a son. My job kept me from being there for them, and I lost them. My wife was a lot like you. She deserved so much more than what I could give her. We divorced when my son was four years old. He's twelve now, and I haven't seen him since he was five. I wish I could tell your husband what it would be like without you. I wish I could take your pain away, because I see my wife's side through you, and it's too late for me to take her pain away. She's married again, had two more children, and she's content. And this makes me happy. I can see you love your husband or you would just leave. You are so strong and stubborn, and I have a feeling you will do what you think is right."

"I'll take you up on that slapping part if needed." We both laughed but his eyes still showed the lingering pain.

"I'm sorry about your family." I put one of my hands on top of his still in my lap. "Can I ask you something?"

"Anything." He looked up to me.

"Why did you choose your job over your family?" I wanted to know, I needed to know why.

"Honestly I don't know. I have been asking myself that for years. I wish I could go back and choose my family, but it's too late. Knowing the consequences from the decision I made would have changed what was more important to me. I miss going home to them, knowing they were always there, just knowing I had a home to go to. I took so much for granted, and I don't want your family to go through the same thing, but I also don't want you to be this unhappy for the rest of your life either." He looked so sad.

"Thank you, Tex, for sharing that with me." I leaned toward him and kissed him on the cheek. "Are you ready for some fun? We are on vacation right?"

The thought of everything we had all been through in the last week wasn't much of a vacation for any of us.

"Are you sure you are up to it?" he asked concerned about my shoulder.

"Are you afraid to lose at poker against a stay-at-home-mom?"

The rest of the team except for Rafael came back out to the deck and sat around the table.

"Bring it on!" Rock said. He poured whiskey in all of our glasses, and I lit the hand rolled cigarette that mysteriously showed up on the table, took a couple of puffs, and handed it to Tex. It made its way around the table, and I finished the last of it.

"So what kind of poker are we playing?" I asked. I had watched it on television many sleepless nights. I knew how to play just about any kind of card game."

"Texas Hold 'Em, of course," Tex stated like there was no other choice.

He winked at me, took a sip from his glass, and started dealing the cards. I looked around the table and felt like I was really a part of something special. Not like a book club or bowling league, not that I was involved in anything like that. It was hard to explain. With the exception of my once a month scrapbooking night, I didn't belong to anything. For the first time in years, I felt like a part of something. I did know the end of this journey was near, and I felt sad and happy at the same time. The conversation with Matt and Hayden kept coming back to my thoughts, and I was struggling to pay attention to the game after a few hands, although I won all three so far. We didn't play for money; I didn't have any. It was nice just to be together and have some laughs. Tex was always telling jokes. I started to wonder how Rafael was doing.

"How is Rafael holding up?" I asked in general not to anyone specifically. The table suddenly got quiet, and I lit a cigarette and took a sip of whiskey.

"He's dealing with a lot right now, but he's strong," Kit answered. I looked directly at Rock, knowing he was closest to Rafael. Rock nodded his head but didn't say anything in response.

"My trip to Panama City Beach and leaving my son for the first time in my life was the most selfish thing I have done. I just wanted some time to myself, and here I've committed adultery and fallen in love with someone I can't have. I'm so sorry. I've been so selfish." I started to cry. The week had finally caught up to me physically and mentally. I felt ashamed of myself. I no longer felt beautiful, and I wondered if it was time to go.

"You're wrong, Maya, this is just another chapter in your life. I can't tell you that you shouldn't feel guilty, but I can tell you that you are an amazing and strong woman. When you go home everything will be the same, and no one will know any different," Rock said reaching across the table to hold my hand.

"No, nothing will ever be the same again." I started to cry harder and Kit handed me a tissue. I wiped my eyes and continued. "I've spent my whole life looking for the kind of love and acceptance you all have given me. The passion Rafael has shared with me will always make me want more. All of you have changed me. I've become very attached to you and I know I can't have it all. I just need to go home and be the best mother I can be, sharing with Hayden all my love and adoration the way you all have shared it with me. That's what I have to hold on to. I know my marriage may never be what I want it to be, but I would never take my son away from his father." I put my head in my hands and cried harder. I went into the bedroom, closed the door, crawled into bed, and cried myself to sleep.

Chapter 24

I woke up and Rafael was asleep behind me with his arms around me. The villa was quiet and the sun was just about to set. I slipped out of bed, went out to the deck, and watched the sun disappear. There was no wind, not even a breeze. The water was still, no waves. There were no birds flying over, not a sound except my own breath. I felt like I was suspended in time and everything just stood still. It was the silence I wasn't used to. Rafael came outside with two glasses of wine.

"I hope I didn't wake you," I muttered.

"No, the loneliness did." He tried to smile but I knew it was difficult.

"Tell me everything that happened today." I took the glass he handed me. I sipped on my wine and waited for him to fill me in.

"If this is all the time I have left with you, I would rather not spend it talking about that." He looked at me seriously.

"Did you at least get some answers about your father?"

"Not really." His face looked drawn, his eyes distant. Obviously he didn't want to talk.

"You know, I think your mother fell in love with him for a reason. Maybe the passion she shared with him was something she kept to herself, something that was just hers. Like you and I. A love so deep she hung on to those memories for the rest of her life. Like I will with you." One lonely tear trickled down my cheek, and he reached for me and pulled me close.

"I heard you finally fell apart today. I'm sorry I wasn't here for you," he said softly in my ear.

"I think everything I kept bubbling down inside me erupted. I'm not as strong as everyone thinks I am. I found out today I'm not even as strong as I thought I was." I pulled away to look at him. I put my hands on both sides of his face and kissed him softly. I never wanted to forget the softness in his lips, the heat of his touch, or the pain we shared in our eyes and our hearts.

"I heard you kicked their asses in poker," he said trying to change the subject.

"When does your boss get here?" I changed the subject again. For all I knew they let me win.

"He'll be here with the team in about a half hour. He wants to meet you."

My face must have shown fear because Rafael smiled and said, "He won't bite you."

"Then I guess I'd better go make myself look presentable." I stood up, kissed Rafael and walked into the bathroom. I put some make up on to cover my puffy eyes, brushed my hair, and struggled to put a sweater over my tank top. I went back outside and sat at the table with Rafael. He had his eyes closed and his head leaning back on the chair. I felt very anxious.

"How is your shoulder?" he asked concerned.

"I'll live, but I could use some aspirin or something. Do you know where they might be?"

"You sit, enjoy your wine, I'll go look. I think the doctor left some pain medication for you."

"Thank you." I smiled with my heart breaking at the same time. He smiled back with the smile that will be imbedded in my heart forever. He looked so handsome in his tan pants and wrinkled white shirt, and I ached to all the times I would never see his hard body and strong face. He came back out with the bottle of pain pills from the doctor, and I took one with my wine. He moved his chair closer to mine and wrapped his arms around me. We sat quietly until we heard the front door open. Rafael stood up and reached for my hand, and we walked into the living room of the villa.

"So this is the infamous Maya?" he said to me, and reached out to shake my hand.

"That would be me. I'm sorry I don't know your name." I felt ignorant.

"This is the head of special operations, Mr. Smith." Rafael introduced him. I giggled a little at the name and then replied, "Encantado, Senor Smith." The team quietly snickered again. I didn't think I'd ever live that down. He smiled at me and had everyone sit down.

"I've gotten an earful about you for the last half hour. I hear you are quite an impressive woman." He sat on the couch next to me with Rafael on the other side.

"They are all liars, Mr. Smith." I looked at Rafael and we exchanged a slight grin.

"I heard you took a bullet for my team." He looked at me seriously and raised an eyebrow.

"I just happened to be in the line of fire. If I could have moved my fat ass out of the way a little quicker, I wouldn't have been hit." I couldn't believe I had just said that.

"May I see your shoulder?" he asked me.

"Now Mr. Smith, what kind of woman would I be to take my shirt off the first time I met a man?" All my wonderful sarcasm was returning, all at once. "I assure you it is fine."

Mr. Smith looked around to the team and then shook his head.

"I see everything I heard was perfectly accurate." He looked back to me and said, "Well it's hard to honor you for your bravery, given you never existed, and for something that never happened. Is there anything we can do for you?"

"Yes, actually, your team hasn't had much of a vacation. I'm sure they could use one after this." There was one other thing I thought he could help me with. "I would like to get into private investigations. If you could give me a recommendation, I would greatly appreciate it." I imagined a letter from the CIA could get me in just about anywhere I wanted.

"Done and done." He smiled in return and then asked, "Would you consider joining my team?"

"I'm afraid I have a four-year-old at home. He's my world and that's where I belong, but I'm more than flattered you would consider me. I appreciate your offer. I have come to love and admire your team very much. They've been like family to me through all of this." I needed to stop there before I started to cry and make a fool of myself again.

"Fair enough. If there is ever anything we can do for you, just let us know." He handed me a card with a handwritten name and number on it.

"Thank you." I reached out to shake his hand, and ended up kissing him on the cheek too. I'm such a sap sometimes. I turned to Rafael and said, "I guess you all have some work to do?" I stood up to excuse myself and Rafael stopped me, "Actually we need to go to the condo for that. Kit is going to stay here with you."

"Okay, but could I talk to you for a minute before you leave?"

"Of course," Rafael said to me then turned to rest of the group. "I'll meet you outside in the car in just a minute."

Mr. Smith and the rest of the team stood up. I went to each of them and hugged and kissed them. When I went to Mr. Smith and hugged him and thanked him for everything, I could tell that he wasn't used to the hugging and kissing by the way he was slightly standoffish. I turned to face them all standing there and tried to imprint each of their faces in my memory.

"Maya, we'll be back later. Maybe we can do a late dinner," Rock said looking at me. I shook my head up and down, but I think he knew I wouldn't be here later when they returned.

"Dinner sounds great. I'll see you all later." They all walked out the door except Kit and Rafael. I took Rafael's hand and walked outside. I couldn't let him know I wouldn't be there later. I hugged him, holding him so tightly I didn't want to let go. I whispered in his ear that I hoped I wasn't a boob in front of his boss, and he laughed. We kissed slowly and sweetly until I knew he had to go.

"I'll be back in a while. Let's cook up some salmon!" he said and turned away, just in time. The tears cascaded down my face uncontrollably.

I walked back inside the villa and sat on the couch. Kit came over and sat next to me. She put her arm around me, and I laid my head on her shoulder. I had to pull myself together.

"Kit, I need to leave before Rafael comes back. I can't say goodbye to him. I just can't do it." I looked at her and she nodded her head in understanding. I got up and went for the pad of paper that was on the counter and went outside. I sat at the table and sipped from my wine still sitting there. I lit a cigarette and starting thinking about what I was going to say to Rafael. Kit came out shortly after with the bottle of wine. She poured herself a glass and refilled mine. I tried to smile but it was so hard. I picked up the pen and started writing.

Rafael,

Please don't be upset at me for leaving this way. If I knew I was kissing you for the last time, I wouldn't want it to end. If I held you, I knew I would never let go. You've given me so much in the last week, and I want to thank you for everything. I lied when I said that I would love you for as long as we were together. I will love you forever. Every time I see the sun, the moon, the beach. Every time I feel the breeze on my face or the sand beneath my feet, I will think of you. The way your skin feels, the way you held me, the way you smell, everything will remind me of you. You've made my heart feel full. My life will never be the same, and I owe you for that. I hope you find love and passion in your life. You deserve to have it all. Please say goodbye to Rock, Tex and Techno for me. I adore them all. Please be safe. The world wouldn't be as beautiful without you in it. I love you, Maya

By the time I finished writing, the paper was wet, the ink blurred. I wasn't sure he'd be able to read it. I folded it up and gave it to Kit.

"Can you make sure he gets this?" I looked at her through the tears.

"Yes," Kit answered quietly.

I took a few minutes to make a mental picture of the view and how gorgeous it was, finished my wine, and stood up.

"Can you call me a cab to take me to the airport?" I asked her with my head down.

"Are you sure this is what you want to do?" she asked me, making sure I hadn't changed my mind.

I nodded yes and grabbed her tightly.

"You've been like a sister to me. Thank you for all that you've done. You will always be in my heart. If there is anything you could call on me for, I will always be a phone call away. Okay?"

She shook her head up and down without saying a word, and I walked into the bathroom to freshen up. I put on the same clothes I came in along with my baseball cap. I had nothing to pack, and when I came out, I saw Kit again. I walked toward her.

"The cab is on the way." She started to cry and I sat next to her. She handed me an envelope.

"What's this?" I asked

"Your poker winnings. Rock wanted you to have it. You'll also need your passport," she said handing it over and smiling wanly. "It should be enough to get you home, and then some." I didn't want to take the winnings, but I had no money or credit card to get home. She poured us another glass of wine and sat with me silently while we waited for the cab.

The horn honked from the driveway and we both stood up. I took one last look at the moon high in the sky and reached for Kit's hand. We walked to the door and I waved to the cab driver. I hugged Kit one more time and walked to the car. As I was getting in, just before I closed the door, Kit said,

"There will be someone waiting for you at the airport to show you to your Jeep." Then she waved goodbye.

"Thank you." I closed the door and waved back.

Chapter 25

I walked into the airport. It was late and quiet. I found a ticket counter and purchased a non-stop flight to Tampa International Airport. My timing couldn't have been better. It was the last flight of the night and leaving in fifteen minutes. I boarded right away and found my seat. I would arrive back in Tampa at three in the morning. I slept most of the way, opening my eyes occasionally and then falling back asleep.

The flight was uneventful, and when I arrived to Tampa, I checked into the hotel at the airport. It was too early to go home now. As I was walking to my room, I remembered that someone was going to meet me, as I heard my name called. There was a man dressed in a suit, unshaven, and looking exhausted walking toward me. I stood still and when he reached me, he handed me my keys and a piece of paper showing where my Jeep was parked. I thanked him and he walked away.

I slept until nine in the morning, checked out and went to a coffee shop downstairs. I was absolutely numb. I didn't deserve to feel anything right now. I took my coffee to go and went in search of my car. It wasn't hard to find. The color alone made it stand out. The top was down just as it had been, and my suitcases were in the back. I got in and started it; my blues music I listened to on the way to Panama City Beach was still on. It almost seemed like nothing had happened.

It was Saturday morning; the sun was bright and warm. The drive home wasn't the same as the drive to the beach condo. I left my home with a feeling of freedom, and now I was returning feeling more empty and alone than before. I couldn't bring myself to think about Rafael yet. It was too painful. I was thinking about how I could work on my marriage and family. I also wondered how my sister was doing and worried about the next time we would see each other. I knew that I wouldn't say anything about what happened, but I also knew that I wasn't going to lie about it. I didn't know what was going to happen in my future, but the memories I'd had in the last week would stay with me forever.

The drive went quickly; it was only about forty five minutes from the airport to my house. When I pulled into the driveway, Hayden and Matt were outside decorating the house with all of our Halloween stuff.

I heard Hayden yell, "Mommy!" I got out of the car and he almost knocked me over with his arms open wide. He was so excited. I picked him up and held him so close. I'd never been away from him before, and had I been sitting in the condo by myself all week, I would have missed him so much more. I was happy to be home and have him in my arms again. I kissed him all over his face and he laughed so hard. Matt walked toward us, and I put my other arm out and we stood holding each other, just the three of us for several minutes. I had to let them both go because the pain in my shoulder was overwhelming.

Matt got my suitcases out of the back of the Jeep, and we all walked into the house. Hayden was talking a mile a minute telling me everything they had done. I just smiled the whole time, enjoying his stories. Matt stood in the kitchen, and as I listened to Hayden, I looked at Matt and we shared another group hug. I still hadn't gotten a word in yet, so finally I asked Matt,

"How was camping?" I smiled because I knew Matt hated the whole tent and cooking by fire thing.

"I'm glad it was only a weekend!" We both laughed.

I turned to Hayden and said,

"How about we go finish the decorations and then we can carve our pumpkin and toast the seeds?" I missed the excitement he had about everything. I never really knew love until the moment he was handed to me.

"Let's do it!" Hayden said jumping up and down.

We had a great day decorating, carving the pumpkin, and getting all the goodie bags together to hand out tomorrow. Hayden and Matt were exhausted by eight o'clock, and Matt was already asleep on the couch when I put Hayden to bed at nine. He didn't engage in any conversation with me, and I wasn't sure if he was just that tired or if he was upset at me.

I took a long bath and for the first time in years, I locked the bathroom door. I needed the privacy. After I cleaned and tended to my shoulder, I put on my favorite pair of pajamas and went to bed by myself. Matt didn't usually come to bed with me. Once he was asleep on the couch, you couldn't wake him up to go to bed. Usually that upset me because I felt like he didn't want to come to bed with me, unless he wanted sex. Then he'd get up. Tonight I wasn't bothered at all. I left him on the couch and curled up in bed and cried myself to sleep.

Hayden woke up early on Sunday in anticipation of Halloween. Whenever Matt had a day off, we let him sleep until he woke up or

Hayden decided it was time around eleven or twelve. Today by ten in the morning, Hayden wanted to go wake him up and share his excitement. He already had his Spider-Man costume on and was ready to go. He never understood the concept of time, but neither did I. It was going to be a long day. When Matt finally woke up, he went into the office and sat at the computer. I brought him in some coffee, which he didn't really drink. On occasion he liked it sweet and on ice.

"Good morning," I said as I handed him the glass and kissed him.

"Hi," he simply stated.

"Did you sleep well?" I asked trying to get him to talk to me.

"Not really." He seemed very short.

"I'm sorry. I'll wait until you're done checking your fantasy football," my smart ass mouth remarked.

"No, I'm sorry, I'm just tired." He turned to face me. "I'm sorry that until now, I haven't appreciated all the things you do around here. It's hard enough just taking care of Hayden. As you can see, I didn't do any laundry or cleaning or anything else for that matter. I see how much you have on your plate, and I'm sorry I don't help you." He sounded heavyhearted and continued, "You have always supported me with anything I've wanted to do, and all the while I've left you home to take care of everything. I've barely had time to think this week much less do all the things you do. I'm sorry that I've been short with you when we have talked. It's just that I've been upset with myself and I'm taking it out on you. I know I do this with work too and I'm so sorry." He was silent for a minute and everything he said caught me off guard.

"Wow. You must have really had a hard week." I smiled at him. "I missed you too. Not the fighting and bickering. I missed the way we used to be. I remember when we first met and all the love and passion we had for each other. I miss that. I think we should continue with our counseling and really work on connecting with each other again. We need to make the time for that." I looked at him tenderly. "It should be the most important thing to us, besides Hayden."

"I agree." He hugged me and I needed to believe the things he said were true and that he wanted to work on our relationship.

"Did the lawyers call about the hearing?" I wondered what the judge decided on our sinkhole case.

"No, but the phone rings off the hook all day long. I really don't know how you keep everything together." He laughed. I wondered what he thought I did all day.

"I'll call them first thing Monday. I bet you're ready to go back to work, huh?" The thought that he had such a rough week, and he didn't realize all that I do was quite amusing.

"YES!" he said enthusiastically.

We spent the rest of the day playing games and trying to keep Hayden busy until it was finally time for trick or treating. When the first young groups started coming to the door, off Hayden and Matt went. I don't usually dress up, but this year I wore Matt's black cloak and his grim reaper mask. It was perfect to hide the tears than came and went for the next few hours. I was happy at about nine when it was time to shut off the outside lights, blow out the candle in the pumpkin, and lock the door.

When they came home, Hayden, regardless of all the candy he ate, was ready for bed. Finally quiet came. Matt went right to the computer. He'd been looking for another job and spent a lot of time putting his resume out there. I couldn't be mad at that. We just weren't spending any time alone, together.

First thing Monday morning, it was back to the grind for all of us. Matt was off to work and I started making all my phone calls. Good news from the lawyer. The judge sided with us on our case, so we were headed to mediation to settle. I spent most of the day catching up on cleaning and laundry, but I found time to play as much as possible with Hayden.

The next few days went on like any other until Thursday. I went out to check the mail, and there was a package addressed to me. I knew I hadn't ordered anything, so I opened it as I walked back to the house. It was the cigarette case that Rafael had given me. The sight of it made me start shaking and I started to cry. I opened the case and there was a note inside.

Maya,
I could never be upset with you. You have given me the most priceless gift of all, your love. My life will never be the same. Thank you for showing me what it means to love and share passion. You are the most amazing woman I'll ever have the pleasure of knowing. You will forever be in my heart and soul. We all miss you already. If fate had anything to do with our paths crossing, maybe we'll meet again someday. I wanted you to keep this gift, though it would never be enough to show how much I love you. I hope you are doing well, and you and your husband make the effort to love again. You will be in my thoughts and prayers. Please don't forget me.
Forever in my heart,
Rafael

I poured a glass of wine and went out on the back porch. I shed a few tears and then realized I had to move on. I scheduled an appointment with our counselor and made a list of all the things I needed to do and work on. I made goals for myself, and for the first time in my life, I was going to make time to do things I needed to do for myself.

The next week I looked into some classes I wanted to take. I wanted to do so many things, mostly work on getting stronger mentally and emotionally first. My shoulder was healing wonderfully, and I was ready to take the stitches out and start strengthening my left arm again. Matt never saw or noticed anything wrong with my shoulder, and I didn't offer any information about it.

I started working out slowly with yoga and some Pilates. Matt and I continued with our counseling, but it seemed the changes he would make only lasted a couple of weeks, and we were back to where we started. I could only work on the things I needed to do, but Matt was still too busy to keep up with the things he was supposed to be working on.

Before I knew it, Thanksgiving was here and Anne-Marie had invited us to their house that year. Both my step-brothers were coming, and she was so happy to have us all together. That was always a problem. With both Matt's family and mine a few miles away, it was always hard. Who's having what holiday and who were we spending each of them with. I loved this time of the year because of Hayden, but hated it at the same time because of all the family dramas.

I was nervous to see my sister for the first time since the week in Panama. I don't think I slept the whole night before, but when we got there she gave me a huge hug and said she loved me. She was never the touchy-feely type, but I lovingly returned the hug and told her how much I loved her too. That day changed our relationship forever; it was an unspoken connection. From that day on, we were friends, not just related. It was something I swore would take a miracle to happen, but something was definitely different between us, and I liked having a sister.

It was about a week-and-a-half later that I received a letter in the mail from the CIA. I couldn't believe it. It said I was extremely qualified to work in a private investigations firm. They were sorry I couldn't be a part of their special ops team and wished me the best. The letter itself was very impressive. I was glowing all day. I hid the letter along with the cigarette case in some old purses I had in the closet. Those secrets were mine and belonged to no one else. It brought the memories back, but mentally, I was much stronger and could smile about that week now without breaking down. It was an adventure and I would never forget it.

We started Hayden in soccer for the fall season. We wanted him to meet new friends and have something that was his own. He loved soccer, and I even enjoyed the other parents sitting on the side. It seemed good for both of us to socialize more. Matt would come to practice after work, and since he worked Saturdays, he would leave work to come to the games and then return to work. He didn't want to miss it, and I was delighted to see him willing to do that for Hayden and me.

The holidays came and went before I could catch my breath. Hayden started pre-Kindergarten after the winter break, and it gave me four hours a day to do whatever I wanted. Of course, for the first few weeks, I cried my four whole hours away until I picked him up. It definitely took some getting used to. Hayden loved school and had no problems adjusting to our new schedule. It was me that had empty nest syndrome for a long time. I was used to always having him with me. For a while I felt more alone than ever, but after a month or so and seeing him so happy, I decided I needed to find happiness also.

I found a trainer that worked with me on self-defense, judo and kick boxing. I trained Monday through Friday for two hours every morning. I was feeling great when March 2nd came. Hayden turned five and I hit the big forty. It was an entire week of celebrations with family and friends. I finally felt good about myself again, doing things for myself and doing things that I had never done but wanted to do. We got a bunch of friends together at a Karaoke bar, and for the first time in my life, I sang in front of a crowded bar. One more thing to check off my "bucket list." Not surprisingly, it took a few glasses of wine to get me up there, but I did it. I sang "Dimming of the Day" by Bonnie Raitt, and at the very end of the song, I could have sworn I saw Rafael in the back of the bar. But when I looked again, he wasn't there. It shook me up a little, but I knew it couldn't have been him. For several days he stayed in my thoughts. I kept wondering if it could have been him, remembering the memories we shared, and happy that in some way I felt he shared this birthday with me.

Matt and I seemed to be doing well with not arguing, and although we still didn't seem to spend any time together, things were happier in our lives. Sometimes I wondered if I just expected him to fill the voids, but now I knew I was responsible for making my life happy. I felt like I was working toward the goals I made for myself, and everyone seemed happier when we were together.

I was in the best shape of my life, loved being a soccer mom, and was proud of the things I was accomplishing. I would call my step-brother who was taking a Spanish class, just to keep up with my own Spanish, and we'd babble on about our lives.

When Hayden was two years old he only spoke one word, Mom, so we did speech therapy and learned sign language so that we could communicate. I started studying that more. Hayden knew seventy-five signs after several weeks of therapy, and it made me laugh because he talked a mile a minute. I had always wanted to continue learning to sign and had added that to my daily routine. Since no one else I knew signed, I did it talking to myself mostly. I didn't know if it was ever something I would need to use, but I liked the fact that I could. You never know. I never thought I would need to know how to defend myself or even speak Spanish for that matter, but look how both came in handy.

My sister and I spent more time together; we even went to the movies, anytime we could sneak away, just the two of us. Even as children, we never did things together. We were always so different and had our own friends and interests. I loved the relationship we were building; it was a shame that it took almost thirty years. Shelby was only two years younger, but we'd never had anything in common, other than our parents, and even then she was my mother's baby, and I was a daddy's girl. It had been harder for Shelby since our mother died. They were so close. I knew that she felt alone not having mom to count on. I think getting closer to each other now had helped her, knowing that she could always count on me.

26
Chapter

Things seemed like they were working for all of us until Matt dropped a huge bomb on me one day. He was offered a job that he wanted so badly, but it meant that he would be traveling on the weekends. He also decided he wanted to go back to school for his masters and found the program he wanted to take online through Colorado State. I thought I was going to fall apart after all the work I'd been doing to feel better about myself. I felt crushed. I felt like we had been getting along so much better, communicating, and even connecting on an emotional level. It had been a very long road to get to this point and now I thought this decision would tear us apart. I'd always supported him and I still would but our marriage would suffer, not to mention how it would affect Hayden.

Summer came and I was so happy to have Hayden home with me. I felt like I was losing him in a way. Everyone says they grow up so fast; I was just learning that now. We spent every moment together. We went to the movies, played outside, and swam in the pool for hours at a time. I couldn't get enough of him knowing school was starting soon and I would be alone again.

Matt accepted his new job that kept him away from home even more. I knew it was important to him, and he really loved what he was doing. I could only hope if he was happier in his own life, he would be happier all around. I continued counseling by myself and tried to conquer each day with all my strength and energy, but when summer came to an end and Hayden started school, everything changed. I fell hard into a downward spiral of depression and wasn't doing anything but crying. I tried to read, treated myself to shopping trips, started back into all the crafts I used to do, and I even went back to my trainer. Nothing seemed to help me out of that funk, until one day I called my dear friend and mentor Kay. We talked for a long time and in the end she said one thing to me. She said I would survive. I always did, no matter how hard things were. I always got through it. That meant so much more than just the words. She had overcome divorce, raising two children alone, and went back to school to become a teacher. When she finally reached the point of gaining her self-worth again, she found the courage to sing a song in a piano bar, "I Will Survive." She sang like she had conquered the world, and no one was ever going to stop her.

I needed that. I wasn't able to talk to anyone about the things I was going through or feeling. Matt and I made a pact years ago that we would never talk to our families about any trouble we were having. I talked with Nana sometimes just about my own feelings and things I was upset about. She was always there for me. Between the two of them, and all of their advice, I knew it was time to make changes for me again. I couldn't sit home anymore feeling sorry for myself; it was time to do something.

The very next day after I got Hayden on the bus to school, I got out the phone book and starting looking for Private Investigative

Firms. I found one fairly close to home, got ready, dug out my letter of recommendation from the CIA, and decided to drop by. I was so nervous, I didn't even tell Matt.

When I opened the doors and went into the building, a beautiful younger woman asked if she could help me. I asked if I could make an appointment to speak to the partners of the firm. Just then, a very well dressed man walked out of his office and saw me speaking to the woman. He walked toward us looking at me from my head to my shoes. When he reached where I was standing, he introduced himself as Mark Meyer, one of the partners of the firm. When I shook his hand he released it and said to the woman that he would talk with me. The way he suspiciously looked at me made me wonder if he thought I was here to see if my husband was cheating on me. I wanted to laugh. I wanted to laugh because Matt actually had an at work wife. He called her, and she would help him with work and personal things, like phone calls and appointments.

He showed me to his office and we sat in the chairs across from his desk.

"How can I help you?" he asked like he knew the answer.

"I'm looking for employment," I stated and handed him the letter of recommendation.

He sat reading the letter and looked up to me in surprise. I wondered what he must have been thinking. He got up from his chair and picked up the phone.

"Can you and Erik come into my office for a minute?" Then he hung up the phone. He turned around to face me and gave me another look over. Just then the two others walked into the office and closed the door behind them. Mark introduced me to them.

"This is my brother Erik and our partner Richard Mack."

I shook each of their hands and said,

"Maya Black, it's very nice to meet you." They both looked to Mark wondering what this was about. He handed them the letter and they both read it. For the few moments of silence in the room, I wondered if I was making a mistake. They nodded to each other and welcomed me to the firm.

"When can you start?" Erik asked me.

"Now sounds good." I smiled the biggest smile I owned; I felt so proud and knew right away this was what I wanted to do.

They invited me to join them for lunch and I happily accepted. I wanted to get to know them as well as what kind of cases they worked on. The firm was in New Tampa, an up and coming area north of Tampa, and was only twenty-five minutes away, so I would be close to home in case Hayden needed me.

Lunch was awesome, not the food, just the company. The three of them looked like calendar models; I could almost picture them posted on a month of the year. I really enjoyed listening to them and their stories. It was a larger firm than I thought; most of the people that worked for them weren't always in the office. We talked about my skills, which really weren't a lot having been a stay-at-home-mom for the last five years. We also discussed my goals, which honestly I hadn't thought about lately, and we discussed where I wanted to be in five years. That was a hard question for me because I could only take one day at a time, but I was honest with them about that.

It went very well and I was impressed by how I handled myself. I told them I wanted to start at the bottom and work my way up. I didn't expect a free pass, so I was willing to do whatever they needed me to do. My only requests were that I needed to be flexible enough to get Hayden on the bus at nine in the morning and be home to get him by four in the afternoon. With Matt home in the evenings, I was willing to work at night if needed.

I imagined that most scandals didn't always happen during the middle of the day.

We went back to the office after lunch and they showed me around, introduced me to my new coworkers, and then the fun stuff. The equipment and devices used for certain jobs was the part that got me really excited. Sometimes they were hired to sweep for devices in big companies protecting sensitive product information. They wanted me for undercover work inside businesses looking for theft or moles. I was so thrilled, and before I realized, it was time for me to get back home.

"I really appreciate this opportunity and I will not let you down." I wanted this.

"We look forward to seeing what you can do." Mark nodded.

The three partners said what a pleasure it was meeting me and that they were happy I was going to be part of their team. They wished me a good night, and I walked out confidently. The afternoon had been a huge success for me, and I couldn't wait to talk to Matt about it.

As I drove home, I could barely contain the excitement. I was so proud of myself. It took me back to the week with Rafael and all the excitement during the week we spent together. I still longed for him, his touch, and his warmth. I wished that I could call him and tell him, but I couldn't. I felt so happy and once again like I had accomplished something spectacular.

I made it home just in time to get to the bus stop, which was only at the corner of our street. Hayden jumped off the bus and ran to me like he usually did and said,

"Mommy you look beautiful. Where did you go today?"

Knowing most days I wore my pajamas all day, he was quick to notice I was all dressed up in a suit and heels.

"Hi, gorgeous. I got a job today, that's why I'm all dressed up. How was your day at school?" I said as we walked back to the house holding hands.

"Great. I met a new friend mom. His name is Zachary!" he said smiling at me. "Where did you get a job, Mom?" he asked and looked at me with a worried face.

"Just in an office, sweetheart. Don't worry, I'll still be here to see you off to school and be right here when you come home," I assured him.

By the time Matt came home, I had dinner ready and was folding a load of never ending laundry. I was still smiling from the day I had, but wanted to wait until Hayden went to bed before I talked to Matt about my new job. I was actually surprised that Hayden didn't tell his father before I did. He was not very good at keeping secrets. He was with me at Christmas time when we went shopping and ended up telling Matt everything we had bought for him before Christmas was even close. I learned not to tell him anything.

Finally, after I cleaned up dinner and watched Matt and Hayden play a few rounds of Star Wars on the Wii, it was time for Hayden to go to bed. Once he was all settled in, I asked Matt if I could talk to him. His face looked concerned. We sat on the couch and I turned down the television so I could have his attention.

"I got a job today." I just blurted it out and smiled.

"Where?"

"Meyer and Mack. It's a PI firm in New Tampa." I waited for his reaction.

"How did you manage that?" he asked like he didn't believe me.

"I just walked in basically and asked for a job. I met with the partners and they thought I would be a great asset." I just stopped there.

"And they just hired you, just like that?"

"You said you would support me in anything I wanted to do. It's not like we haven't talked about this before. Why are you so surprised that I could get this kind of job?" I started to feel defensive. We had talked about my finding a job when Hayden started school many times.

"I'm not surprised, just…." He paused not finishing what he was going to say.

"Don't worry, it won't affect my duties as mother and wife." I could tell that he didn't like the idea, although whenever we talked about my going in to private investigations, he said he supported me. I wondered if it was because he thought I would never really do it. My anger started building, and I just stared at him. I had been so excited, and he always had this way of raining on my parade.

"Anyway, I started today, and can't wait to go back tomorrow." I stood up and went to the kitchen to pour a glass of wine. Matt didn't say anything else. I heard him turn up the volume on the television and start flipping through the channels. I assumed our conversation was over.

I took my wine out on the porch and sat looking at our backyard. I needed to clean the pool and cut back some bushes. Matt never said anything else that night about my new job, not that it mattered, but I was hoping for a "way to go" or "congratulations, I'm happy for you," something along that line.

By the time I came in the house, Matt was already asleep on the couch. I went in to take a bath, got ready for bed, and went to turn down the volume on Hayden's t.v. He always slept with the television on. I covered him up and kissed him goodnight, then crawled into bed by myself. I could barely sleep thinking about what tomorrow would be like at my new job.

The mornings would be a little more chaotic having to get Hayden and myself ready at the same time so that I could leave after he was on the bus, but everything worked out fine.

I arrived at the firm by nine-thirty and walked into the building. The woman that I talked to yesterday was at the desk,

"Good morning, Maya." she said and I smiled at her.

"Good morning, Megan. How was your evening?" I asked her after reading her name on a plaque. She was so sweet and in a small way reminded me of Kit.

"Wonderful. Thank you for asking. Mark would like to see you in his office." She stood up and walked me to his office door. She knocked and then opened it for me. I walked inside and Mark stood up and came to shake my hand.

"Good morning. I wanted to show you something before we get started today," he said as I followed him out of his office and down the hall. He opened a door and walked in.

"This will be your office; we'll get you set up later with anything you need. What do you think?" He turned around looking at the room and then back to me.

"Thank you. I don't know what to say. I wasn't expecting my own office." I was stunned. It was painted in a deep shade of taupe with white trim. The desk was mahogany with a black leather chair. I just looked around the room for a minute and then back to Mark.

Most of the employees didn't come to the office; they received their assignments via fax or mail and worked in the field or from home.

"I called Mr. Smith last night and we talked quite a while about you. I hope you don't mind that I called to check your reference. I had a meeting with Erik and Richard this morning, and we would like you to be based here and work with us on some of our bigger cases. If that's alright with you?" He waited for me to respond.

"Yes. Thank you again for this opportunity." I wondered what Mr. Smith had said to him.

"Great. I thought you might want to work with Richard today. He has a sweep to do and a simple surveillance job. I'll let you get settled, and Richard will let you know when he is ready to go," he said as he walked out the door. I stood there, baffled. Was I dreaming this? It just didn't seem real.

I sat down at my desk and put my purse down. I turned my chair to look out the window and my eyes filled with tears. I will survive. I sat there lost in my thoughts when I heard a knock on the door. I turned around to see Richard standing at the door.

"Ready?" he asked.

"Ready," I replied.

Within the first few minutes, I knew this day was going to be a lot of fun. Richard was very laid back, and it didn't take me long to figure out he was unhappy with his home life. I didn't ask any questions; I tried to just listen. We arrived at the client's office and walked in together. Richard and I were shown around to the offices that needed to be checked and were left alone. He showed me the device they used and how to read it, but mostly I just watched with an eagle eye and note pad.

Richard found one device in the conference room.

"Now we take it back to the office and trace it. We can get a little information on where it was purchased, maybe who. Then we write a report on our findings and send the bill to the company. Easy," he informed me.

When we were back in the car and on the road, I asked as many questions that I could think of. I felt like a Bounty paper towel trying to absorb as much as I could. The next thing I knew we were sitting in a parking lot of another office building. Richard pulled out a file with a photo of a man, the make and model of his car, and we sat waiting for him to come out.

"How are you with a camera?" he asked me.

"Excellent." I was proud of the fact that I had a great camera. Matt had bought me a Nikon with all kinds of lenses depending on what was needed. In scrapbooking, the photo was the most important thing, so the camera made all the difference.

We saw the man come out and get in his car. Richard handed me the camera.

"It's all yours."

I started shooting photos of him in his car as we followed him. We stopped at a restaurant about ten minutes away. The man got out of his car and entered the restaurant. I snapped photos until he was inside.

"Are you hungry?" I asked Richard.

"I could eat," he replied, curious of what I had in mind.

We went inside and sat at the table behind the man we followed. I made sure the flash was off on the camera and set it on my lap. We looked at the menus, then set them down. Our waitress came over and Richard ordered a glass of wine, so I did the same. He was facing the door and I was facing our subject. Richard started making small talk while we waited to see who our subject was meeting. Just then, a woman came in and walked right to the table we were watching. The man stood up, kissed her, then pulled out a chair for her. I knew already that the woman was not his wife.

"Is this a cheating husband case?" I asked Richard.

"What was your first clue?"

I didn't know him well enough to know if he was being sarcastic or serious.

"For one, he pulled the chair out for her," I laughed. I acted like I was taking a picture of Richard and caught them just when they were kissing. They never saw a thing. I took a sip of my wine, but my attention was intently on our two subjects. What surprised me was that the couple didn't even look suspicious or the least bit afraid someone might see them.

"What do you see?" Richard had his back to them so he was counting on me for information, or testing me, I wasn't sure.

"Is the wife out of town?" I asked him.

"Yes. What made you ask that?"

"They aren't afraid to be seen. They seem excited to be in public together, somewhere other than behind closed doors, and they haven't looked over their shoulders one time to see if anyone was watching them." I looked back to Richard and took another sip of my wine.

"Well, I think we should get going then." He finished his wine.

"That's it?" I asked.

"All we needed was proof. We'll fill out a report when we get back, print the photos, and call in the client." He smiled like he loved what he did and made it sound so simple. Richard paid the bill for our drinks, and we left the restaurant. I checked the pictures as soon as we got in the car to make sure they came out well. They were perfect.

"I'll bring my camera in on Monday and keep it in the office." I looked at him and he nodded.

We got back to the office building, and I followed him to his office so we could do the paperwork. The report was the most important thing. We noted the times, locations, details of the meeting, everything that was a fact. No opinions, just the facts. This case was very simple. Richard told me earlier that he had followed a man for two weeks before he got any proof.

Mark walked into the office and asked how things went, not expecting us to be back so soon.

"She's a natural!" Richard answered.

Mark looked at me and asked if I had a gun and license to carry a concealed weapon.

"No, that's one thing I haven't trained in, but I have a shooting range a few miles from my house," I commented, thinking how I passed it every time I went to the tanning salon.

"Great, since its Friday, why don't you take next week and train, get yourself a gun and license and spend as much time at the range as you can." He seemed to think I would really enjoy that. I had never even held a gun before much less shot one. I'd never liked guns and I certainly wasn't going to keep it at home. I smiled at Mark and said,

"I look forward to it."

"I'll finish up here, I'm sure it's time for you to get going," Richard said to me.

I looked at the clock on the wall and it was time for me to leave.

"Thank you for everything, I had a great day. I guess I will see you in a week then. I hope you both have a great weekend and I look forward to next week at the range." I smiled and walked to my office to grab my purse and headed out.

"Have a great weekend, Megan." I said to her on my way out.

"You too, Maya," she replied.

Chapter 27

On my way home I started thinking about my new job. I had really had a great day. I was in a wonderful mood when I got home. Hayden had a great day at school, and even when Matt came home as I was cooking dinner, he kissed me and said he had a great day too. I think this is going to work out, I thought.

We spent the weekend together going to the park, playing by the pool, and cooking on the grill. Matt even helped with cutting those bushes in the backyard while I cleaned the pool. We all seemed really happy together and had such a wholesome weekend. Sunday night, after Hayden had gone to bed, Matt sat next to me on the couch and we talked for a long time. We still weren't talking about my job, but I felt closer to him than I had in a very long time. He even went to bed with me that night. We made love for the first time in months, and I felt like we were connecting again. Men never understood that women wanted sex to satisfy an emotional need, while men wanted sex for the physical need. We fell asleep in each other's arms.

I was a little nervous about the firing range, so first thing Monday morning, I called my dad.

"Hi, baby," he answered. I loved that he still called me that. I hadn't had a chance since I started my new job to call and tell him all about it.

"Hi, daddy. I need a big favor," I said.

"What's up?" he asked.

"Can you meet me at the firing range on Ridge Road in about thirty minutes? I'll explain everything when you get there," I told him. If there was anyone I wanted to teach me about guns, it would be him. He was in the military and had always had quite a collection of guns and rifles, which he showed to Matt while he was asking for my hand in marriage. It was just like my dad to do something like that.

"Okay." I could hear the confusion in his voice.

"I'll see you there. I love you," I said smiling to myself.

"Love you too, baby," he said and hung up the phone.

As soon as the bus came and Hayden was on his way, I hopped in the Jeep and headed to the firing range. My dad pulled in right next to me, and I waited for him to get out.

After a big hug and kiss, I explained to him about my job and what I was doing and that I needed to learn how to use a gun, purchase one of my own, and get a license to carry a concealed weapon. I'll never forget the smile he had on his face.

"Well let's see what you got," he said walking toward the door to the building. I followed behind him giggling like a little girl. We walked inside, and my dad knew the guy working there from one of the motorcycle groups he rode with. We explained to him that I needed to learn to shoot and get a license to carry.

Julio, choose a few different kinds of guns, and we walked through another set of sound proof doors. He grabbed some ear plugs and set the guns down on the platform. He put a paper target on a line and sent it out about fifty feet. He gave me the first gun, showed me what to do, and told me to go ahead and fire. My first shot missed the target completely. Fueled by my own competitiveness, I shot five more times and hit the outer edge of the target. I tried the next gun. It was much heavier and I had a hard time with the aim. The third one was perfect. It fit my hand, it wasn't too heavy, and I hit the bull's eye each time. I looked to my dad who was smiling. I took the earplugs out and asked,

"What's so funny?"

"You are definitely my daughter!" He laughed.

I put the earplugs in and reloaded the gun. It was a 38 snub-nose revolver, only a six shot, but semi-automatic, so I could shoot rapidly. After a few more targets, I was ready to go. I purchased the gun all chromed out with a mother of pearl handle, as well as thigh and ankle holsters. It was small enough to carry in my purse, but in case I needed to wear it, I wanted to have the right accessories. I filled out the application, had my fingerprints taken, and signed up for the required safety class the next day. After a background check, the license would come in the mail. I was happy to get through all of that in one day.

The next day, I took the safety class and then spent two hours practicing. The rest of my day went quickly using the time to catch up on some things around the house. I made brownies for Hayden for a treat when he came home. Matt even came home early from work, and we all ate dinner together and played some games on the Wii. I sat on the couch and stared at both of them. I loved them so much and I felt so happy.

By Thursday, I was as good with my left hand shooting as I was my right and so proud of myself. I wanted to climb the stairs to a large building while listening to the Rocky theme song. I felt triumphant.

After I left the range, I decided to go to the firm and check in. I brought my targets with me.

Megan greeted me with a smile and I asked if the guys were in.

"Actually, they are in the conference room. Go on in," she replied. I walked down the hall and knocked on the door,

"Come in, Maya" They could see me from the row of windows before the door.

I opened the door and walked in and sat down with them.

"How has your week been?" I asked looking at all three of them.

"It's been pretty quiet here. How was your week at the range?" Erik asked.

I handed them my targets from today.

"Impressive, for someone who has never shot a gun before. What are the L and R in the corners?" Mark asked.

"Left and right handed." I simply stated, thinking "duh". The look on their faces was priceless. I tried hard to control my laughter at their reaction.

"You are a better shot than the three of us together!" Richard commented, and they all laughed.

"I just have to wait for my license to come in the mail. Is it okay if I keep it locked in my office?" I asked, not wanting to keep it at home.

"Absolutely. We'll have a safe put in your desk drawer," Mark was quick to reply.

"We were just talking about taking tomorrow off; we weren't expecting to see you until Monday, so feel free to take a long weekend," Erik said.

"Okay," I nodded and stood up. I had plenty I could be doing at home. Finally settling on our sinkhole lawsuit, I had all kinds of fixing to do. I started to walk to the door and Mark said,

"Maya, don't you want your paycheck?"

"For what, I haven't even done anything yet." I was confused.

"Let's just call it training pay," he commented as he walked with me to his office and handed me an envelope.

"Thank you. I wasn't expecting this."

"Maybe it will cover the cost of the range and gun. We are really happy to have you on our team. We just wanted to make sure that you know how much we appreciate you. We take very good care of our own." He smiled and held his hand out to shake mine. I felt like I should hug him, but I shook his hand and said thank you. I waved to Erik and Richard saying "Have a good weekend and see you on Monday." I headed out after saying the same to Megan and drove home, singing the whole way.

When I pulled into the garage and closed the door behind me, I sat in the Jeep and opened the envelope. The check was for two thousand dollars. I almost pissed in my pants. I was sure that it was a mistake. I didn't know what private investigators made, and we had never talked about pay. It never mattered to me; I hadn't earned a paycheck in over five years. I started to cry. This was all so emotional for me. I had accomplished everything I had written down for goals. Now I felt like I could live the rest of my life and feel successful as a mother, wife, and a woman.

On Friday, I wanted to just relax, soak in the tub, and lounge around the house. I was pouring a glass of wine when the phone rang; it was around lunch time so I was guessing it was Matt, but I didn't look at the caller ID.

"Hello," I answered.

"Maya."

I grabbed the kitchen counter for support, feeling like I was going to fall down. My heart started beating so hard I could feel myself shaking. I turned around and slid down the back of my kitchen cabinets until I was sitting on the floor. I felt like I couldn't breathe.

"Rafael?"